Dracula's Precursors

DAVID ANNWN, poet and critic, teaches for the Open University. His essays include "Returning to Fear: Discoveries in Robertson's Fantasmagoria" (*The New Magic Lantern,* 2008), "Dazzling Ghostland, Sheridan Le Fanu's Phantasmagoria" (*Irish Journal of Gothic and Horror Studies,* 2009) and "The Gnome's Lighted Scrolls: Consumerism & Pre-Cinematic Visual Technologies in Doctor Jekyll and Mr Hyde" (*Journal of Stevenson Studies,* 2010). *Gothic Machine: Textualities, Pre-cinematic Media and Film in Popular Visual Culture 1670-1910* is forthcoming from the University of Wales Press, 2011.

Dracula's Precursors:
The Mysterious Stranger
& other stories

RESCRIPT BOOKS

ReScript Books is an imprint of
REALITY STREET
63 All Saints Street, Hastings TN34 3BN
www.realitystreet.co.uk/rescript-books.php

Cover illustration: *The Vampire* by Sir Philip Burne-Jones
Original texts courtesy of www.litgothic.com

Printed & bound in Great Britain
by Lightning Source UK Ltd

First ReScript Books edition, 2011

A catalogue record for this book is available from the British Library

ISBN: 978-1-874400-49-3

Introduction..7

The Mysterious Stranger
by Anonymous..13

The Last Lords of Gardonal
by William Gilbert 57

Let Loose
by Mary Cholmondeley 99

Introduction

Given that "The Mysterious Stranger" (1823), long out of print, is the best, most chilling and finely-realised of *Dracula*'s literary precursors—Byron's *The Giaour* (1813) is a sketch and *Varney the Vampire* (1845-7) a baggy monster in comparison—this present edition is an extremely welcome addition to the literary annals of vampirism.

Stoker enthusiasts, both those new to "The Mysterious Stranger" and others attracted again by its re-appearance in book form, will find this anonymously-penned tale is rewarding, particularly in the ways that it anticipates so many of the motifs of *Dracula*. The story's opening with a journey to the east into the Carpathian Mountains, the vampire's immense strength, noble status and power over wolves, and the hunting by night are all familiar. The vampire, Ezzelin von Klatka, like Dracula, sleeps in his coffin in the crypt of a ruined chapel and subsists on blood. He too is vulnerable to staking. Woislaw, the savant of vampiric activity, may even have inspired the character of Van Helsing.

Set early in the 17th century, the opening of the tale finds an Austrian ruler, the Knight of Fahnenberg, his companion, the Baron Franz von Kronstein, a "fine young man", their guide and a litter containing his daughter Franziska and his niece Bertha travelling deep into the eastern wilds, in order to take possession of his inherited lands. Sexual tensions and marital dilemmas underpin this as well as the other two vampire tales included here. Anticipating the love-travails of Mina and Lucy in *Dracula*, Franziska is scornful of her courtship by cousin Franz, described as a "pretty" and "effeminate" man. Anxieties about potency and gender cluster in the young people's exchanges in the blizzard-swept cavalcade and, indeed, the title itself proleptically hints at Franziska's need to encounter the racially and sexually other, entirely removed from her perceptions of Germanic dullness. Yet it is her relation, Bertha, the staid Teuton, who urges her to accept Franz's suit, who will be proved right. Pan-Germanism will win the day over that eastern wildness which ultimately threatens to drain Franziska to a husk.

The narrative is well-turned and the windswept terrain of the forested mountain country is established with a vivid detail. Clever devices, such as the ingenious strength of Woislaw's golden hand which will outwit Ezzelin, are unique to this tale. There is also a lively humour at play in, for example, the knowing wink to the reader when Ezzelin, assured that he won't be evicted from his dilapidated chapel, says that "people of my sort are rather difficult to turn out". The quality of the English translation (first published in *Odds and Ends*), is fluent and engaging, in comparison to the stiffness of many Englished versions of the *Schauer*/Shudder and *Rauber*/Robber novels that started to proliferate in Britain after the success of Schiller's *Der Geisterseher* (1789).

As in the case of Peter Teuthold's translation of Karl Friedrich Kahlert's *The Necromancer* (1794), these narratives frequently dealt with the activities of noblemen caught up in war and legends of bandits concealed in ruined castles, keeping the locals away with tales of ghosts. This is the reason that Ezzelin's castle is said to be a "robber's den" and why the haughty vampire lord scathingly insists: "Yes; but, nevertheless, I have no communication with robbers…"

The other major influence evident in this work is that line of particularly fervid German writing associated with horrifying revenants, stemming from Gottfried Burger's ballad, "Lenora", through Goethe's "The Bride of Corinth" (1797), to J L Tieck's "Wake Not the Dead" (1819), the last of these translated into English in 1823, the year of "The Mysterious Stranger"'s original appearance. As this strain of erotic supernaturalism emerges into the 1820s, the potentially lethal power of women becomes a dominant theme in these and related works. For example, in Tieck's story, Brunhilda, wife of a nobleman who revives her from death, reveals her new dominance by draining him entirely of his blood.

Franziska von Fahnenberg is revealed as a worthy inheritor of this unswerving female strength: it is she who yearns for Carpathian wildness, craves a mate worthy of her unruly desires and finds Ezzelin's callous arrogance and nocturnal hunting so thrilling. She is also forced to face her deepest fears in effecting her own release from Ezzelin's control. These themes anticipate the ideas of "The New Woman" in *Dracula* by over seventy years. For critics who have noted homosexual tensions in Dracula's preference for enrolling young males, rather than women, into his vampiric clan, Ezzelin, in the midst of his admiration of Franziska's charms as a woman, expressly wishes she were a man. For those gender and sexual anxieties particularly rife in the 1890s to be encoded in a work originally penned in the 1820s is remarkable.

In "The Last Lords of Gardonal" (1867), first published in *Argosy* and written by William Gilbert, the father of the famous D'Oyly Carte librettist, it is a passionate love for the Italian farmer's vulnerable daughter, Teresa Biffi, which drags the Swiss despot, Conrad, to his own catastrophic encounter with the undead. He will win the young woman as his bride at long last but only to face a magician's wrath and a nightly assault on his body, the latter mirroring his own original intentions of ambush and rape for the girl. Each of the three stories feature the familiar Gothic motif of cruel and exploitative roués who prey upon the ordinary inhabitants of their hereditary domains. In two, this is the vampire himself; in "The Last Lords..." the erstwhile despot ultimately becomes the victim of his own lust and a moral intelligence much greater than his own. In an uncanny pre-visioning of the Mexican farmers in the film *The Magnificent Seven* (1960), the desperate Lombard farmers, reeling with the injustices committed against them by Conrad's riders, enlist the help of *Il Innominato*, or the Nameless One, a magician whose exploits became the basis for an anthology of tales by Gilbert.

The sudden switch from an impassive and objective-seeming prose detailing Conrad and his men's successive outrages against the villagers to the very direct account of the intimate, nightly counter-rape of Conrad by his intended victim still inspires a real shudder. The Germanic notion of woman empowered as vampire re-asserts itself here and there is something haunting about the transformation of Teresa, in her resurrected form, from her oblivious daytime sweetness to her nocturnal guise as an unassuageable blood-sucker. This tale is also a very unusual literary example of vampirism sanctioned in terms of moral revenge which marks a new development in Victorian thought about the uses of horror.

It is, again, a sexual mystery and questions surrounding marriage which instigate the tale within the tale of "Let Loose" (1890). The narrator cannot fathom his new brother-in-law's "certain quiet power of overcoming obstacles", and particularly the source of his attraction exerted over his family in the face of obvious hostility:

> …my parents did not like him much and opposed the marriage, and my sister did not like him at all, and refused him over and over again; but, nevertheless, he eventually married her.

As in the case of the other tales, the hidden answer is bound up in the tale of Blake the brother-in-law's youthful journey to an unfamiliar territory, in this case the Yorkshire wolds, where vistas of dykes, long treeless tracks and grey houses with "primitive" inhabitants open out.

Leading up to one of the most frightening episodes, a local clergyman warns Blake against marriage but, despite initial resistance, finally agrees to let him into the closed crypt which contains a rare fresco. Handing him the keys which have been locked away in an oak cupboard, the minister warns:

> "Likewise," he added, "be careful that you lock the first door at the foot of the steps before you unlock the second, and lock the second also while you are within. Furthermore, when you come out lock the iron inner door as well as the wooden one."

Each clause in this verbal itinerary freights the different stages of Blake's descent into the crypt with further dread; when he walks into the crypt it's as if he's entering a Freudian strong-box containing the repressed nightmares of a community, the slowing of pace and proliferation of detail only intensifying the feeling of intimate menace. The ironic juxtaposition of the Ascension mural with Sir Roger Despard's cursing of the angels operates as effectively as the neatly arranged *memento mori* among the tombs.

The generally laconic tone of the narration and demotic title, "Let Loose", remind one of the masterworks of M R James; and the account of the solitary traveller looking into old secrets best left well alone in remote churches strongly prefigures "Canon Alberic's Scrapbook" four years later. Cholmondeley's story was popular and, though she encountered charges of plagiarism, those who looked for influences in, for example, F G Loring's "The Tomb of Sara" (1900), were confounded by the former tale's much earlier date. In any case, the dark, sardonic wit and understatement of Cholmondeley's tale clearly stem from the same source as that of her best-seller, *Red Pottage* (1890).

Despite the fabulous subject matter of each tale, great emphasis is placed on period, landscape and seasonal setting. In "The Mysterious Stranger", Fahrenberg reaches the Carpathians in April and hails forth from lower Austria at the time of the Habsburg expansion into Hungary during the "Long War" (1593-1606). This tale reveals what seems to be a first-hand, or at least good reading knowledge of the Carpathian landscape and fauna. The description of the mountain winds mixing sand and gravel and throwing them into the eyes of the travellers rings as authentic. The reference to golden jackals, (*Canis aureus moreoticus*) as "reed-wolves" reveals familiarity with the denizens of eastern European forests.

The action of "The Last Lords..." spans from the Engadin valley of the Swiss alps in the canton of Graubünden to Bormio in the Valtelline valley in Lombardy. Gilbert's tale tracks through mountainscapes using real place-names to the extent that one can follow his journey on a modern map. The depredations of his immoral brigands are planned in cognizance of and limited by the seasonal blocking of the high mountain routes.

The setting of "Let Loose" is the fictional Wet Waste-on-the-Wolds (Wetwang?), near Pickering, and the story perhaps blends the High and Low Marishes a few miles to the south, the Pickering church-frescoes and the Saxon crypt at Lastingham. One of the tales from William of Newburgh's *Historia Rerum Anglicarum* (circa 1198) tells of a vampire, the spirit of a wealthy man, roving the streets of a hamlet barked at by dogs. Newburgh Priory, William's home, was situated in the wolds and perhaps it was the reference to canine distubance which gave Mary Cholmondeley the idea for the story's ending. For the writers of all three tales employ animals as influential agencies in the narratives. The reed wolves help herd the travellers toward Ezzelin. The Innominato's magical bird proves Conrad's nemesis in controlling and punishing the dissolute lord. Perhaps a post-Monty Python audience may find a canine called Brian difficult to take seriously, but in "Let Loose" it is this creature that is most alive to the invisible threat impinging upon the community and his master's life. Cholmondeley has used the Gelert legend of the faithful dog mistakenly killed for protecting his charge to give the ending of her tale a real sense of regret and lurking evil. The deeper the final lines sink into the reader's mind, the more they realise their terrifying future implications for Blake's listener and his unsuspecting sister.

The setting and mood of "The Mysterious Stranger" were to influence Jules Verne's *The Carpathian Castle* (1893, filmed in 1981), as dramatically as they did those of *Dracula*. For his own part, Ezzelin von Klatka had warned readers that he was difficult to eject and, indeed, he crops up by name in various publications, including, most recently in Kim Newman's *Anno Dracula* (1992).

Taken collectively and in relation to that which recent research has revealed to be a spacious domain of pre-Dracula literary works, these tales represent three of the very best antecedents to Stoker's tale gathered together here for the first time.

David Annwn, June 2010

The Mysterious Stranger
by Anonymous
(translated from the German)

"To die? to sleep!
Perchance to dream? Ay, there's the rub." — *Hamlet.*

B oreas, that fearful north-west wind, which in the spring and autumn stirs up the lowest depths of the wild Adriatic, and is then so dangerous to vessels, was howling through the woods, and tossing the branches of the old knotty oaks in the Carpathian Mountains, when a party of five riders, who surrounded a litter drawn by a pair of mules, turned into a forest-path, which offered some protection from the April weather, and allowed the travellers in some degree to recover their breath. It was already evening, and bitterly cold; the snow fell every now and then in large flakes. A tall old gentleman, of aristocratic appearance, rode at the head of the troop. This was the Knight of Fahnenberg, in Austria. He had inherited from a childless brother a considerable property, situated in the Carpathian Mountains; and he had set out to take possession of it, accompanied by his daughter Franziska, and a niece about twenty years of age, who had been brought up with her. Next to the knight rode a fine young man some twenty and odd years—the Baron Franz von Kronstein; he wore, like the former, the broad-brimmed hat with hanging feathers, the leather collar, the wide riding-boots—in short, the travelling-dress which was in fashion at the commencement of the seventeenth century. The features of the young man had much about them that was open and friendly, as well as some mind; but the expression was more that of dreamy and sensitive softness than of youthful daring, although no one could deny that he possessed much of youthful beauty. As the cavalcade turned into the oak wood the young man rode up to the litter, and chatted with the ladies who were seated therein. One of these—and to her his conversation was principally addressed—was of dazzling beauty. Her hair flowed in natural curls round the fine oval of her face, out of which beamed a pair of star-like eyes, full of genius, lively fancy, and a certain degree of archness. Franziska von Fahnenberg seemed to attend but carelessly to the speeches of her admirer, who made many kind inquiries as to how she felt herself during the journey, which had been attended with many difficulties: she always answered him very shortly; almost contemptuously; and at length remarked, that if it had not been for her father's objections, she would long ago have requested the baron to take her place in their horrid cage of a litter, for, to judge by his remarks, he seemed incommoded by the weather; and she would so much rather be mounted on the spirited horse, and face wind and storm, than be mewed up there, dragged up the hills by those long-eared animals, and mope herself to death with ennui. The young lady's words, and, still more, the half-contemptuous tone in which they were uttered, appeared to make the most painful impression on the young man: he made her no reply at the moment, but the absent air with which he attended to the kindly-intended remarks of the other young lady, showed how much he was disconcerted.

"It appears, dear Franziska," said he at length in a kindly tone, "that the hardships of the road have affected you more than you will acknowledge. Generally so kind to others, you have been very often out of humour during the journey, and particularly with regard to your humble servant and cousin, who would gladly bear a double or treble share of the discomforts, if he could thereby save you from the smallest of them."

Franziska showed by her look that she was about to reply with some bitter jibe, when the voice of the knight was heard calling for his nephew, who galloped off at the sound.

"I should like to scold you well, Franziska," said her companion somewhat sharply, "for always plaguing your poor Cousin Franz in this shameful way; he who loves you so truly, and who, whatever you may say, will one day be your husband."

"My husband!" replied the other angrily. "I must either completely alter my ideas, or he his whole self, before that takes place. No, Bertha! I know that this is my father's darling wish, and I do not deny the good qualities Cousin Franz may have, or really has, since I see you are making a face; but to marry an effeminate man—never!"

"Effeminate! you do him great injustice," replied her friend quickly. "Just because instead of going off to the Turkish war, where little honour was to be gained, he attended to your father's advice, and stayed at home, to bring his neglected estate into order, which he accomplished with care and prudence; and because he does not represent this howling wind as a mild zephyr—for reasons such as these you are pleased to call him effeminate."

"Say what you will, it is so," cried Franziska obstinately. "Bold, aspiring, even despotic, must be the man who is to gain my heart; these soft, patient, and thoughtful natures are utterly distasteful to me. Is Franz capable of deep sympathy, either in joy or sorrow? He is always the same—always quiet, soft and tiresome."

"He has a warm heart, and is not without genius," said Bertha.

"A warm heart! that may be," replied the other; "but I would rather be tyrannized over, and kept under a little by my future husband, than be loved in such a wearisome manner. You say he has genius, too. I will not exactly contradict you, since that would be unpolite, but it is not easily discovered. But even allowing you are right in both statements, still the man who does not bring these qualities into action is a despicable creature. A man may do many foolish things, he may even be a little wicked now and then, provided it is in nothing dishonourable; and one can forgive him, if he is only acting on some fixed theory for some special object. There is, for instance, your own faithful admirer, the Castellan of Glogau, Knight of Woislaw; he loves you most truly, and is now quite in a position to enable you to marry comfortably. The brave man has lost his right hand—reason enough for remaining seated behind the stove, or near the spinning-wheel of his Bertha; but what does he do?—He goes off to the war in Turkey; he fights for a noble thought—"

"And runs the chance of getting his other hand chopped off, and another great scar across his face," put in her friend.

"Leaves his lady-love to weep and pine a little," pursued Franziska, "but returns with fame, marries, and is all the more honoured and admired! This is done by a man of forty, a rough warrior, not bred at court, a soldier who has nothing but his cloak and sword. And Franz—rich, noble—but I will not go on. Not a word more on this detested point, if you love me, Bertha."

Franziska leaned back in the corner of the litter with a dissatisfied air, and shut her eyes as though, overcome by fatigue, she wished to sleep.

"This awful wind is so powerful, you say, that we must make a detour to avoid its full force," said the knight to an old man, dressed in a fur-cap and a cloak of rough skin, who seemed to be the guide of the party.

"Those who have never personally felt the Boreas storming over the country between Sessano and Triest, can have no conception of the reality," replied the other. "As soon as it commences, the snow is blown in thick long columns along the ground. That is nothing to what follows. These columns become higher and higher, as the wind rises, and continue to do so until you see nothing but snow above, below, and on every side—unless, indeed, sometimes, when sand and gravel are mixed with the snow, and at length it is impossible to open your eyes at all. Your only plan for safety is to wrap your cloak around you, and lie down flat on the ground. If your home were but a few hundred yards off, you might lose your life in the attempt to reach it."

"Well, then, we owe you thanks, old Kumpan," said the knight, though it was with difficulty he made his words heard above the roaring of the storm; "we owe you thanks for taking us this round, as we shall thus be enabled to reach our destination without danger."

"You may feel sure of that, noble sir," said the old man. "By midnight we shall have arrived, and that without any danger by the way, if—" Suddenly the old man stopped, he drew his horse sharply up, and remained in an attitude of attentive listening.

"It appears to me we must be in the neighbourhood of some village," said Franz von Kronstein; "for between the gusts of the storm I hear a dog howling."

"It is no dog, it is no dog!" said the old man uneasily, and urging his horse to a rapid pace. "For miles around there is no human dwelling; and except in the castle of Klatka, which indeed lies in the neighbourhood, but has been deserted for more than a century, probably no one has lived here since the creation.—But there again," he continued; "well, if I wasn't sure of it from the first."

"That howling seems to fidget you, old Kumpan," said the knight, listening to a long-drawn fierce sound, which appeared nearer than before, and seemed to be answered from a distance.

"That howling comes from no dogs," replied the old guide uneasily. "Those are reed-wolves; they may be on our track; and it would be as well if the gentlemen looked to their firearms."

"Reed-wolves ? What do you mean?" inquired Franz in surprise.

"At the edge of this wood," said Kumpan, "there lies a lake about a mile long, whose banks are covered with reeds. In these a number of wolves have taken up their quarters, and feed on wild birds, fish and such like. They are shy in the summer-time, and a boy of twelve might scare them; but when the birds migrate, and the fish are frozen up, they prowl about at night, and then they are dangerous. They are worst, however, when Boreas rages, for then it is just as if the fiend himself possessed them: they are so mad and fierce that man and beast become alike their victims; and a party of them have been known even to attack the ferocious bears of these mountains, and, what is more, to come off victorious." The howl was now again repeated more distinctly, and from two opposite directions. The riders in alarm felt for their pistols, and the old man grasped the spear which hung at his saddle.

"We must keep close to the litter; the wolves are very near us," whispered the guide. The riders turned their horses, surrounded the litter, and the knight informed the ladies, in a few quieting words, of the cause of this movement.

"Then we shall have an adventure—some little variety!" cried Franziska with sparkling eyes.

"How can you talk so foolishly?" said Bertha in alarm.

"Are we not under manly protection? Is not Cousin Franz on our side?" said the other mockingly.

"See, there is a light gleaming among the twigs; and there is another," cried Bertha. "There must be people close to us."

"No, no," cried the guide quickly. "Shut up the door, ladies. Keep close together, gentlemen. It is the eyes of wolves you see sparkling there." The gentlemen looked towards the thick underwood, in which every now and then little bright spots appeared, such as in summer would have been taken for glow-worms; it was just the same greenish-yellow light, but less unsteady, and there were always two flames together. The horses began to be restive, they kicked and dragged at the rein; but the mules behaved tolerably well.

"I will fire on the beasts, and teach them to keep their distance," said Franz, pointing to the spot where the lights were thickest.

"Hold, hold, Sir Baron!" cried Kumpan quickly, and seizing the young man's arm. "You would bring such a host together by the report, that, encouraged by numbers, they would be sure to make the first assault. However, keep your arms in readiness, and if an old she-wolf springs out—for these always lead the attack—take good aim and kill her, for then there must be no further hesitation." By this time the horses were almost unmanageable, and terror had also infected the mules. Just as Franz was turning towards the litter to say a word to his cousin, an animal, about the size of a large hound, sprang from the thicket and seized the foremost mule.

"Fire, baron! A wolf! " shouted the guide.

The young man fired, and the wolf fell to the ground. A fearful howl rang through the wood.

"Now, forward! Forward without a moment's delay!" cried Kumpan. "We have not above five minutes' time. The beasts will tear their wounded comrade to pieces, and, if they are very hungry, partially devour her. We shall, in the meantime, gain a little start, and it is not more than an hour's ride to the end of the forest. There—do you see—these are the towers of Klatka between the trees—out there where the moon is rising, and from that point the wood becomes less dense."

The travellers endeavoured to increase their pace to the utmost, but the litter retarded their progress. Bertha was weeping with fear, and even Franziska's courage had diminished, for she sat very still. Franz endeavoured to reassure them. They had not proceeded many moments when the howling recommenced, and approached nearer and nearer.

"There they are again and fiercer and more numerous than before," cried the guide in alarm.

The lights were soon visible again, and certainly in greater numbers. The wood had already become less thick, and the snowstorm having ceased, the moonbeams discovered many a dusky form amongst the trees, keeping together like a pack of hounds, and advancing nearer and nearer till they were within twenty paces, and on the very path of the travellers. From time to time a fierce howl arose from their centre, which was answered by the whole pack, and was at length taken up by single voices in the distance.

The party now found themselves some few hundred yards from the ruined castle of which Kumpan had spoken. It was, or seemed by moonlight to be, of some magnitude. Near the tolerably preserved principal building lay the ruins of a church, which must have once been beautiful, placed on a little hillock, dotted with single oak-trees and bramble-bushes. Both castle and church were still partially roofed in; and a path led from the castle gate to an old oak-tree, where it joined at right angles the one along which the travellers were advancing. The old guide seemed in much perplexity.

"We are in great danger, noble sir," said he. "The wolves will very soon make a general attack. There will then be only one way of escape: leaving the mules to their fate, and taking the young ladies on your horses."

"That would be all very well, if I had not thought of a better plan," replied the knight. "Here is the ruined castle; we can surely reach that, and then, blocking up the gates, we must just await the morning."

"Here? In the ruins of Klatka?— Not for all the wolves in the world!" cried the old man. "Even by daylight no one likes to approach the place, and, now, by night!— The castle, Sir Knight, has a bad name."

"On account of robbers?" asked Franz.

"No; it is haunted," replied the other.

"Stuff and nonsense!" said the baron. "Forward to the ruins; there is not a moment to be lost."

And this was indeed the case. The ferocious beasts were but a few steps behind the travellers. Every now and then they retired, and set up a ferocious howl. The party had just arrived at the old oak before mentioned, and were about to turn into the path to the ruins, when the animals, as though perceiving the risk they ran of losing their prey, came so near that a lance could easily have struck them. The knight and Franz faced sharply about, spurring their horses amidst the advancing crowds, when suddenly, from the shadow of the oak stepped forth a man, who in a few strides placed himself between the travellers and their pursuers. As far as one could see in the dusky light, the stranger was a man of a tall and well-built frame; he wore a sword by his side, and a broad-brimmed hat was on his head. If the party were astonished at his sudden appearance, they were still more so at what followed. As soon as the stranger appeared, the wolves gave over their pursuit, rumbled over each other, and set up a fearful howl. The stranger now raised his hand, appeared to wave it, and the wild animals crawled back into the thickets like a pack of beaten hounds.

Without casting a glance at the travellers, who were too much overcome by astonishment to speak, the stranger went up the path which led to the castle, and soon disappeared beneath the gateway.

"Heaven have mercy on us!" murmured old Kumpan in his beard, as he made the sign of the cross.

"Who was that strange man?" asked the knight with surprise, when he had watched the stranger as long as he was visible, and the party had resumed their way.

The old guide pretended not to understand, and, riding up to the mules, busied himself with arranging the harness, which had become disordered in their haste: more than a quarter of an hour elapsed before he rejoined them.

"Did you know the man who met us near the ruins, and who freed us from our four-footed pursuers in such a miraculous way?" asked Franz of the guide.

"Do I know him? No, noble sir; I never saw him before," replied the guide hesitatingly. "He looked like a soldier, and was armed," said the baron. "Is the castle, then, inhabited?"

"Not for the last hundred years," replied the other. "It was dismantled because the possessor in those days had iniquitous dealings with some Turkish-Sclavonian hordes, who had advanced as far as this; or rather"—he corrected himself hastily—"he is said to have had such, for he might have been as upright and good a man as ever ate cheese fried in butter."

"And who is now the possessor of the ruins and of these woods?" inquired the knight.

"Who but yourself, noble sir?" replied Kumpan. "For more than two hours we have been on your estate, and we shall soon reach the end of the wood."

"We hear and see nothing more of the wolves," said the baron after a pause. "Even their howling has ceased. The adventure with the stranger still remains to me inexplicable, even if one were to suppose him a huntsman—"

"Yes, yes; that is most likely what he is," interrupted the guide hastily, whilst he looked uneasily round him.

"The brave good man, who came so opportunely to our assistance, must have been a huntsman Oh, there are many powerful woodsmen in this neighbourhood! Heaven be praised!" he continued, taking a deep breath, "there is the end of the wood, and in a short hour we shall be safely housed."

And so it happened. Before an hour had elapsed, the party passed through a well-built village, the principal spot on the estate, towards the venerable castle, the windows of which were brightly illuminated, and at the door stood the steward and other dependents, who, having received their new lord with every expression of respect, conducted the party to the splendidly furnished apartments.

Nearly four weeks passed before the travelling adventures again came on the tapis. The knight and Franz found such constant employment in looking over all the particulars of the large estate, and endeavouring to introduce various German improvements, that they were very little at home. At first, Franziska was charmed with everything in a neighbourhood so entirely new and unknown. It appeared to her so romantic, so very different from her German Fatherland, that she took the greatest interest in everything, and often drew comparisons between the countries, which generally ended unfavourably for Germany. Bertha was of exactly the contrary opinion: she laughed at her cousin, and said that her liking for novelty and strange sights must indeed have come to a pass, when she preferred hovels in which the smoke went out of the doors and windows instead of the chimney, walls covered with soot, and inhabitants not much cleaner, and of unmannerly habits, to the comfortable dwellings and polite people of Germany. However, Franziska persisted in her notions, and replied that everything in Austria was flat, ennuyant, and common; and that a wild peasant here, with his rough coat of skin, had ten times more interest for her than a quiet Austrian in his holiday suit, the mere sight of whom was enough to make one yawn.

As soon as the knight had got the first arrangements into some degree of order, the party found themselves more together again. Franz continued to show great attention to his cousin, which, however, she received with little gratitude, for she made him the butt of all her fanciful humours, that soon returned when after a longer sojourn she had become more accustomed to her new life. Many excursions into the neighbourhood were undertaken, but there was little variety in the scenery, and these soon ceased to amuse.

The party were one day assembled in the old-fashioned hall, dinner had just been removed, and they were arranging in which direction they should ride. "I have it," cried Franziska suddenly, "I wonder we never thought before of going to view by day the spot where we fell in with our night-adventure with wolves and the Mysterious Stranger."

"You mean a visit to the ruins—what were they called?" said the knight.

"Castle Klatka," cried Franziska gaily. "Oh, we really must ride there! It will be so charming to go over again by daylight, and in safety, the ground where we had such a dreadful fright."

"Bring round the horses," said the knight to a servant "and tell the steward to come to me immediately." The latter, an old man, soon after entered the room.

"We intend taking a ride to Klatka," said the knight: "we had an adventure there on our road."

"So old Kumpan told me," interrupted the steward.

"And what do you say about it?" asked the knight.

"I really don't know what to say," replied the old man, shaking his head. "I was a youth of twenty when I first came to this castle, and now my hair is grey; half a century has elapsed during that time. Hundreds of times my duty has called me into the neighbourhood of those ruins, but never have I seen the Fiend of Klatka."

"What do you say? Whom do you call by that name?" inquired Franziska, whose love of adventure and romance was strongly awakened.

"Why, people call by that name the ghost or spirit who is supposed to haunt the ruins," replied the steward. "They say he only shows himself on moonlight nights —"

"That is quite natural," interrupted Franz smiling. "Ghosts can never bear the light of day; and if the moon did not shine, how could the ghost be seen? for it is not supposed that any one for a mere freak would visit the ruins by torch-light."

"There are some credulous people who pretend to have seen this ghost," continued the steward. "Huntsmen and wood-cutters say they have met him by the large oak on the cross-path. That, noble sir, is supposed to be the spot he inclines most to haunt, for the tree was planted in remembrance of the man who fell there."

"And who was he?" asked Franziska with increasing curiosity.

"The last owner of the castle, which at that time was a sort of robber's den, and the headquarters of all depredators in the neighbourhood," answered the old man. "They say this man was of superhuman strength, and was feared not only on account of his passionate temper, but of his treaties with the Turkish hordes. Any young woman, too, in the neighbourhood to whom he took a fancy, was carried off to his tower and never heard of more. When the measure of his iniquity was full, the whole neighbourhood rose in a mass, besieged his stronghold, and at length he was slain on the spot where the huge oak-tree now stands."

"I wonder they did not burn the whole castle, so as to erase the very memory of it," said the knight.

"It was a dependency of the church, and that saved it," replied the other. "Your great-grandfather afterwards took possession of it, for it had fine lands attached. As the Knight of Klatka was of good family, a monument was erected to him in the church, which now lies as much in ruin as the castle itself."

"Oh, let us set off at once! Nothing shall prevent my visiting so interesting a spot," said Franziska eagerly. "The imprisoned damsels who never reappeared, the storming of the tower, the death of the knight, the nightly wanderings of his spirit round the old oak, and, lastly, our own adventure, all draw me thither with an indescribable curiosity."

When a servant announced that the horses were at the door, the young girls tripped laughingly down the steps which led to the coach-yard. Franz, the knight, and a servant well acquainted with the country, followed; and in a few minutes the party were on their road to the forest.

The sun was still high in the heavens when they saw the towers of Klatka rising above the trees. Everything in the wood was still, except the cheerful twitterings of the birds as they hopped about amongst the bursting buds and leaves, and announced that spring had arrived.

The party soon found themselves near the old oak at the bottom of the hill on which stood the towers, still imposing in their ruin. Ivy and bramble bushes had wound themselves over the walls, and forced deep roots so firmly between the stones that they in a great measure held these together. On the top of the highest spot, a small bush in its young fresh verdure swayed lightly in the breeze.

The gentlemen assisted their companions to alight, and leaving the horses to the care of the servant, ascended the hill to the castle. After having explored this in every nook and cranny, and spent much time in a vain search for some trace of the extraordinary stranger, whom Franziska declared she was determined to discover, they proceeded to an inspection of the adjoining church. This they found to have better withstood the ravages of time and weather; the nave, indeed, was in complete dilapidation, but the chancel and altar were still under roof, as well as a sort of chapel which appeared to have been a place of honour for the families of the old knights of the castle. Few traces remained, however, of the magnificent painted glass which must once have adorned the windows, and the wind entered at pleasure through the open spaces.

The party were occupied for some time in deciphering the inscriptions on a number of tombstones, and on the walls, principally within the chancel. They were generally memorials of the ancient lords, with figures of men in armour, and women and children of all ages. A flying raven and various other devices were placed at the corners. One gravestone, which stood close to the entrance of the chancel, differed widely from the others: there was no figure sculptured on it, and the inscription, which, on all besides, was a mere mass of flattering eulogies, was here simple and unadorned; it contained only these words: "Ezzelin von Klatka fell like a knight at the storming of the castle"—on such a day and year.

"That must be the monument of the knight whose ghost is said to haunt these ruins," cried Franziska eagerly.

"What a pity he is not represented in the same way as the others—I should so like to have known what he was like!"

"Oh, there is the family vault, with steps leading down to it, and the sun is lighting it up through a crevice, said Franz, stepping from the adjoining vestry.

The whole party followed him down the eight or nine steps which led to a tolerably airy chamber, where were placed a number of coffins of all sizes, some of them crumbling into dust. Here, again, one close to the door was distinguished from the others by the simplicity of its design, the freshness of its appearance, and the brief inscription: "Ezzelinus de Klatka, Eques."

As not the slightest effluvium was perceptible, they lingered some time in the vault; and when they reascended to the church, they had a long talk over the old possessors, of whom the knight now remembered he had heard his parents speak. The sun had disappeared, and the moon was just rising as the explorers turned to leave the ruins. Bertha had made a step into the nave, when she uttered a slight exclamation of fear and surprise. Her eyes fell on a man who wore a hat with drooping feathers, a sword at his side, and a short cloak of somewhat old-fashioned cut over his shoulders. The stranger leaned carelessly on a broken column at the entrance; he did not appear to take any notice of the party; and the moon shone full on his pale face.

The party advanced towards the stranger.

"If I am not mistaken," commenced the knight; "we have met before."

Not a word from the unknown.

"You released us in an almost miraculous manner," said Franziska, "from the power of those dreadful wolves. Am I wrong in supposing it is to you we are indebted for that great service?"

"The beasts are afraid of me," replied the stranger in a deep fierce tone, while he fastened his sunken eyes on the girl, without taking any notice of the others.

"Then you are probably a huntsman," said Franz, "and wage war against the fierce brutes."

"Who is not either the pursuer or the pursued? All persecute or are persecuted, and Fate persecutes all," replied the stranger without looking at him.

"Do you live in these ruins?" asked the knight hesitatingly.

"Yes; but not to the destruction of your game, as you may fear, Knight of Fahnenberg," said the unknown contemptuously. "Be quite assured your property shall remain untouched—"

"Oh! my father did not mean that," interrupted Franziska, who appeared to take the liveliest interest in the stranger. "Unfortunate events and sad experiences have, no doubt, induced you to take up your abode in these ruins, of which my father would by no means dispossess you."

"Your father is very good, if that is what he meant," said the stranger in his former tone; and it seemed as though his dark features were drawn into a slight smile; "but people of my sort are rather difficult to turn out."

"You must live very uncomfortably here," said Franziska, half vexed, for she thought her polite speech had deserved a better reply.

"My dwelling is not exactly uncomfortable, only somewhat small, still quite suitable for quiet people," said the unknown with a kind of sneer. "I am not, however, always quiet; I sometimes pine to quit the narrow space, and then I dash away through forest and field, over hill and dale; and the time when I must return to my little dwelling always comes too soon for me."

"As you now and then leave your dwelling," said the knight, "I would invite you to visit us, if I knew——"

"That I was in a station to admit of your doing so," interrupted the other; and the knight started slightly, for the stranger had exactly expressed the half-formed thought. "I lament," he continued coldly, "that I am not able to give you particulars on this point—some difficulties stand in the way: be assured, however, that I am a knight, and of at least as ancient a family as yourself."

"Then you must not refuse our request," cried Franziska, highly interested in the strange manners of the unknown. "You must come and visit us."

"I am no boon-companion, and on that account few have invited me of late," replied the other with his peculiar smile; "besides, I generally remain at home during the day; that is my time for rest. I belong, you must know, to that class of persons who turn day into night, and night into day, and who love everything uncommon and peculiar."

"Really? So do I! And for that reason, you must visit us," cried Franziska. "Now," she continued smiling, "I suppose you have just risen, and you are taking your morning airing. Well, since the moon is your sun, pray pay a frequent visit to our castle by the light of its rays. I think we shall agree very well, and that it will be very nice for us to be acquainted."

"You wish it?— You press the invitation?" asked the stranger earnestly and decidedly.

"To be sure, for otherwise you will not come," replied the young lady shortly.

"Well, then, come I will!', said the other, again fixing his gaze on her. " If my company does not please you at any time, you will have yourself to blame for an acquaintance with one who seldom forces himself, but is difficult to shake off."

When the unknown had concluded these words, he made a slight motion with his hand, as though to take leave of them, and passing under the doorway, disappeared among the ruins. The party soon after mounted their horses, and took the road home.

It was the evening of the following day, and all were again seated in the hall of the castle. Bertha had that day received good news. The knight Woislaw had written from Hungary, that the war with the Turks would be brought to a conclusion during the year, and that although he had intended returning to Silesia, hearing of the knight of Fahnenberg having gone to take possession of his new estates, he should follow the family there, not doubting that Bertha had accompanied her friend. He hinted that he stood so high in the opinion of his duke on account of his valuable services, that in future his duties would be even more important and extensive; but before settling down to them, he should come and claim Bertha's promise to become his wife. He had been much enriched by his master, as well as by booty taken from the Turks. Having formerly lost his right hand in the duke's service, he had essayed to fight with his left; but this did not succeed very admirably, and so he had an iron one made by a very clever artist. This hand performed many of the functions of a natural one, but there had been still much wanting; now, however, his master had presented him with one of gold, an extraordinary work of art, produced by a celebrated Italian mechanic. The knight described it as something marvellous, especially as to the superhuman strength with which it enabled him to use the sword and lance. Franziska naturally rejoiced in the happiness of her friend, who had had no news of her betrothed for a long time before. She launched out every now and then, partly to plague Franz, and partly to express her own feelings, in the highest praise and admiration of the bravery and enterprise of the knight, whose adventurous qualities she lauded to the skies. Even the scar on his face, and his want of a right hand, were reckoned as virtues; and Franziska at last saucily declared that a rather ugly man was infinitely more attractive to her than a handsome one, for as a general rule handsome men were conceited and effeminate. Thus, she added, no one could term their acquaintance of the night before handsome, but attractive and interesting he certainly was. Franz and Bertha simultaneously denied this. His gloomy appearance, the deadly hue of his complexion, the tone of his voice, were each in turn depreciated by Bertha, while Franz found fault with the contempt and arrogance obvious in his speech. The knight stood between the two parties. He thought there was something in his bearing that spoke of good family, though much could not be said for his politeness; however, the man might have had trials enough in his life to make him misanthropical. Whilst they were conversing in this way, the door suddenly opened, and the subject of their remarks himself walked in.

"Pardon me, Sir Knight," he said coldly, "that I come, if not uninvited, at least unannounced; there was no one in the antechamber to do me that service."

The brilliantly lighted chamber gave a full view of the stranger. He was a man about forty, tall, and extremely thin. His features could not be termed uninteresting—there lay in them something bold and daring; but the expression was on the whole anything but benevolent. There was contempt and sarcasm in the cold grey eyes, whose glance, however, was at times so piercing, that no one could endure it long. His complexion was even more peculiar than the features: it could neither be called pale nor yellow; it was a sort of grey, or, so to speak, dirty white, like that of an Indian who has been suffering long from fever; and was rendered still more remarkable by the intense blackness of his beard and short cropped hair. The dress of the unknown was knightly, but old-fashioned and neglected; there were great spots of rust on the collar and breastplate of his armour; and his dagger and the hilt of his finely-worked sword were marked in some places with mildew. As the party were just going to supper, it was only natural to invite the stranger to partake of it; he complied, however, only in so far that he seated himself at the table, for he ate no morsel. The knight, with surprise, inquired the reason.

"For a long time past, I have accustomed myself never to eat at night," he replied with a strange smile. "My digestion is quite unused to solids, and indeed would scarcely confront them. I live entirely on liquids."

"Oh, then, we can empty a bumper of Rhine-wine together," cried the host.

"Thanks; but I neither drink wine nor any cold beverage," replied the other; and his tone was full of mockery. It appeared as if there was some amusing association connected with the idea.

"Then I will order you a cup of hippocras"—a warm drink composed of herbs—"it shall be ready immediately," said Franziska.

"Many thanks, fair lady; not at present," replied the other. "But if I refuse the beverage you offer me now, you may be assured that as soon as I require it—perhaps very soon—I will request that, or some other of you."

Bertha and Franz thought the man had something inexpressibly repulsive in his whole manner, and they had no inclination to engage him in conversation; but the baron, thinking that perhaps politeness required him to say something, turned towards the guest, and commenced in a friendly tone: "It is now many weeks since we first became acquainted with you; we then had to thank you for a signal service—"

"And I have not yet told you my name, although you would gladly know it," interrupted the other dryly. "I am called Azzo; and as"—this he said again with his ironical smile—"with the permission of the Knight of Fahnenberg, I live at the castle of Klatka, you can in future call me Azzo von Klatka."

"I only wonder you do not feel lonely and uncomfortable amongst those old walls," began Bertha. "I cannot understand —"

"What my business is there? Oh, about that I will willingly give you some information, since you and the young gentleman there takes such a kindly interest in my person," replied the unknown in his tone of sarcasm.

Franz and Bertha both started, for he had revealed their thoughts as though he could read their souls. "You see, lady," he continued, "there are a variety of strange whims in the world. As I have already said, I love what is peculiar and uncommon, at least what would appear so to you. It is wrong in the main to be aston-ished at anything, for, viewed in one light, all things are alike; even life and death, this side of the grave and the other, have more resemblance than you would imagine. You perhaps consider me rather touched a little in my mind, for taking up my abode with the bat and the owl; but if so, why not consider every hermit and recluse insane? You will tell me that those are holy men. I certainly have no pretension that way; but as they find pleasure in praying and singing psalms, so I amuse myself with hunting. Oh, you can have no idea of the intense pleasure of dashing away in the pale moonlight, on a horse that never tires, over hill and dale, through forest and woodland! I rush among the wolves, which fly at my approach, as you yourself perceived, as though they were puppies fearful of the lash."

"But still it must be lonely, very lonely for you," remarked Bertha.

"So it would by day; but I am then asleep," replied the stranger dryly; "at night I am merry enough."

"You hunt in an extraordinary way," remarked Franz hesitat-ingly.

"Yes; but, nevertheless, I have no communication with robbers, as you seem to imagine," replied Azzo coldly.

Franz again started—that very thought had just crossed his mind. "Oh, I beg your pardon; I do not know —" he stammered.

"What to make of me," interrupted the other. "You would, therefore, do well to believe just what I tell you, or at least to avoid making conjectures of your own, which will lead to nothing."

"I understand you: I know how to value your ideas, if no one else does," cried Franziska eagerly. "The humdrum, everyday life of the generality of men is repulsive to you; you have tasted the joys and pleasures of life, at least what are so called, and you have found them tame and hollow. How soon one tires of the things one sees all around! Life consists in change. Only in what is new, uncommon, and peculiar, do the flowers of the spirit bloom and give forth scent. Even pain may become a pleasure if it saves one from the shallow monotony of everyday life—a thing I shall hate till the hour of my death."

"Right, fair lady—quite right! Remain in this mind: this was always my opinion, and the one from which I have derived the highest reward," cried Azzo; and his fierce eyes sparkled more intensely than ever. "I am doubly pleased to have found in you a person who shares my ideas. Oh, if you were a man, you would make me a splendid companion; but even a woman may have fine experiences when once these opinions take root in her, and bring forth action!"

As Azzo spoke these words in a cold tone of politeness, he turned from the subject, and for the rest of his visit only gave the knight monosyllabic replies to his inquiries, taking leave before the table was cleared. To an invitation from the knight, backed by a still more pressing one from Franziska to repeat his visit, he replied that he would take advantage of their kindness, and come sometimes.

When the stranger had departed, many were the remarks made on his appearance and general deportment. Franz declared his most decided dislike to him. Whether it was as usual to vex her cousin, or whether Azzo had really made an impression on her, Franziska took his part vehemently. As Franz contradicted her more eagerly than usual, the young lady launched out into still stronger expressions; and there is no knowing what hard words her cousin might have received had not a servant entered the room.

The following morning Franziska lay longer than usual in bed.

When her friend went to her room, fearful lest she should be ill, she found her pale and exhausted. Franziska complained she had passed a very bad night; she thought the dispute with Franz about the stranger must have excited her greatly, for she felt quite feverish and exhausted, and a strange dream, too, had worried her, which was evidently a consequence of the evening's conversation. Bertha, as usual, took the young man's part, and added, that a common dispute about a man whom no one knew, and about whom any one might form his own opinion, could not possibly have thrown her into her present state. "At least," she continued, "you can let me hear this wonderful dream."

To her surprise; Franziska for a length of time refused to do so.

"Come, tell me," inquired Bertha, "what can possibly prevent you from relating a dream—a mere dream? I might almost think it credible, if the idea were not too horrid, that poor Franz is not very far wrong when he says that the thin, corpse-like, dried-up, old-fashioned stranger has made a greater impression on you than you will allow."

"Did Franz say so?" asked Franziska. "Then you can tell him he is not mistaken. Yes, the thin, corpse-like, dried-up, whimsical stranger is far more interesting to me than the rosy-checked, well-dressed, polite, and prosy cousin."

Strange," cried Bertha. "I cannot at all comprehend the almost magic influence which this man, so repulsive, exercises over you."

"Perhaps the very reason I take his part, may be that you are all so prejudiced against him," remarked Franziska pettishly. "Yes, it must be so; for that his appearance should please my eyes, is what no one in his senses could imagine. But," she continued, smiling and holding out her hand to Bertha, "is it not laughable that I should get out of temper even with you about this stranger?— I can more easily understand it with Franz—and that this unknown should spoil my morning, as he has already spoiled my evening and my night's rest?"

"By that dream, you mean?" said Bertha, easily appeased, as she put her arm round her cousin's neck and kissed her. "Now, do tell it to me. You know how I delight in hearing anything of the kind."

"Well, I will, as a sort of compensation for my peevishness towards you," said the other, clasping her friend's hands. "Now, listen! I had walked up and down my room for a long time; I was excited—out of spirits—I do not know exactly what. It was almost midnight ere I lay down, but I could not sleep. I tossed about, and at length it was only from sheer exhaustion that I dropped off. But what a sleep it was! An inward fear ran through me perpetually. I saw a number of pictures before me, as I used to do in childish sicknesses. I do not know whether I was asleep or half awake. Then I dreamed, but as dearly as if I had been wide awake, that a sort of mist filled the room, and out of it stepped the knight Azzo. He gazed at me for a time, and then letting himself slowly down on one knee, imprinted a kiss on my throat. Long did his lips rest there; and I felt a slight pain, which always went on increasing, until I could bear it no more. With all my strength I tried to force the vision from me, but succeeded only after a long struggle. No doubt I uttered a scream, for that awoke me from my trance. when I came a little to my senses, I felt a sort of superstitious fear creeping over me—how great you may imagine when I tell you that, with my eyes open and awake, it appeared to me as if Azzo's figure were still by my bed, and then disappearing gradually into the mist, vanished at the door!"

"You must have dreamed very heavily, my poor friend," began Bertha, but suddenly paused. She gazed with surprise at Franziska's throat. "Why, what is that?" she cried. " Just look: how extraordinary—a red streak on your throat!"

Franziska raised herself, and went to a little glass that stood in the window. She really saw a small red line about an inch long on her neck, which began to smart when she touched it with her finger.

"I must have hurt myself by some means in my sleep," she said after a pause; "and that in some measure will account for my dream."

The friends continued chatting for some time about this singular coincidence—the dream and the stranger; and at length it was all turned into a joke by Bertha.

Several weeks passed. The knight had found the estate and affairs in greater disorder than he at first imagined; and instead of remaining three or four weeks, as was originally intended, their departure was deferred to an indefinite period. This postponement was likewise in some measure occasioned by Franziska's continued indisposition. She who had formerly bloomed like a rose in its young fresh beauty, was becoming daily thinner, more sickly and exhausted, and at the same time so pale, that in the space of a month not a tinge of red was perceptible on the once glowing cheek. The knight's anxiety about her was extreme, and the best advice was procured which the age and country afforded; but all to no purpose. Franziska complained from time to time that the horrible dream with which her illness commenced was repeated, and that always on the day following she felt an increased and indescribable weakness. Bertha naturally set this down to the effect of fever, but the ravages of that fever on the usually dear reason of her friend filled her with alarm.

The knight Azzo repeated his visits every now and then. He always came in the evening, and when the moon shone brightly. His manner was always the same. He spoke in monosyllables, and was coldly polite to the knight; to Franz and Bertha, particularly to the former, contemptuous and haughty; but to Franziska, friendliness itself. Often when, after a short visit, he again left the house, his peculiarities became the subject of conversation. Besides his old way of speaking, in which Bertha said there lay a deep hatred, a cold detestation of all mankind with the exception of Franziska, two other singularities were observable. During none of his visits, which often took place at supper-time, had he been prevailed upon to eat or drink anything, and that without giving any good reason for his abstinence. A remarkable alteration, too, had taken place in his appearance; he seemed an entirely different creature. The skin, before so shrivelled and stretched, seemed smooth and soft, while a slight tinge of red appeared in his cheeks, which began to look round and plump. Bertha, who could not at all conceal her ill-will towards him, said often, that much as she hated his face before, when it was more like a death's-head than a human being's, it was now more than ever repulsive; she always felt a shudder run through her veins whenever his sharp piercing eyes rested on her. Perhaps it was owing to Franziska's partiality, or to the knight Azzo's own contemptuous way of replying to Franz, or to his haughty way of treating him in general, that made the young man dislike him more and more. It was quite observable, that whenever Franz made a remark to his cousin in the presence of Azzo, the latter would immediately throw some ill-natured light on it, or distort it to a totally different meaning. This increased from day to day, and at last Franz declared to Bertha, that he would stand such conduct no longer, and that it was only out of consideration for Franziska that he had not already called him to account.

At this time the party at the castle was increased by the arrival of Bertha's long-expected guest. He came just as they were sitting down to supper one evening, and all jumped up to greet their old friend. The knight Woislaw was a true model of the soldier, hardened and strengthened by war with men and elements. His face would not have been termed ugly, if a Turkish sabre had not left a mark running from the right eye to the left cheek, and standing out bright red from the sunburned skin. The frame of the Castellan of Glogau might almost be termed colossal. Few would have been able to carry his armour, and still fewer move with his lightness and ease under its weight. He did not think little of this same armour, for it had been a present from the palatine of Hungary on his leaving the camp. The blue wrought-steel was ornamented all over with patterns in gold; and he had put it on to do honour to his bride-elect, together with the wonderful gold hand, the gift of the duke. Woislaw was questioned by the knight and Franz on all the concerns of the campaign; and he entered into the most minute particulars relating to the battles, which, with regard to plunder, had been more successful than ever. He spoke much of the strength of the Turks in a hand-to-hand fight, and remarked that he owed the duke many thanks for his splendid gift, for in consequence of its strength many of the enemy regarded him as something superhuman. The sickliness and deathlike paleness of Franziska was too perceptible not to be immediately noticed by Woislaw; accustomed to see her so fresh and cheerful, he hastened to inquire into the cause of the change. Bertha related all that had happened, and Woislaw listened with the greatest interest. This increased to the utmost at the account of the often-repeated dream, and Franziska had to give him the most minute particulars of it; it appeared as though he had met with a similar case before, or at least had heard of one. When the young lady added, that it was very remarkable that the wound on her throat which she had at first felt had never healed, and still pained her, the knight Woislaw looked at Bertha as much as to say, that this last fact had greatly strengthened his idea as to the cause of Franziska's illness.

It was only natural that the discourse should next turn to the knight Azzo, about whom every one began to talk eagerly. Woislaw inquired as minutely as he had done with regard to Franziska's illness, about what concerned this stranger, from the first evening of their acquaintance down to his last visit, without, however, giving any opinion on the subject. The party were still in earnest conversation, when the door opened, and Azzo entered. Woislaw's eyes remained fixed on him, as he, without taking any particular notice of the new arrival, walked up to the table, and seating himself, directed most of the conversation to Franziska and her father, and now and then made some sarcastic remark when Franz began to speak. The Turkish war again came on the tapis, and though Azzo only put in an occasional remark, Woislaw had much to say on the subject. Thus they had advanced late into the night, and Franz said smiling to Woislaw: "I should not wonder if day had surprised us, whilst listening to your entertaining adventures."

"I admire the young gentleman's taste," said Azzo, with an ironical curl of the lip. "Stories of storm and shipwreck are, indeed, best heard on terra firma, and those of battle and death at a hospitable table or in the chimney-corner. One had then the comfortable feeling of keeping a whole skin, and being in no danger, not even of taking cold." With the last words, he gave a hoarse laugh, and turning his back on Franz, rose, bowed to the rest of the company, and left the room. The knight, who always accompanied Azzo to the door, now expressed himself fatigued, and bade his friends good night.

"That Azzo's impertinence is unbearable," cried Bertha when he was gone. "He becomes daily more rough, unpolite, and presuming. If only on account of Franziska's dream, though of course he cannot help that, I detest him. Now, tonight, not one civil word has he spoken to any one but Franziska, except, perhaps, some casual remark to my uncle."

"I cannot deny that you are right, Bertha," said her cousin. "One may forgive much to a man whom fate had probably made somewhat misanthropical; but he should not overstep the bounds of common politeness. But where on earth is Franz?" added Franziska, as she looked uneasily round.—The young man had quietly left the room whilst Bertha was speaking.

"He cannot have followed the knight Azzo to challenge him?" cried Bertha in alarm.

"It were better he entered a lion's den to pull his mane!" said Woislaw vehemently. "I must follow him instantly," he added, as he rushed from the room.

He hastened over the threshold, out of the castle, and through the court, before he came up to them. Here a narrow bridge with a slight balustrade passed over the moat by which the castle was surrounded. It appeared that Franz had only just addressed Azzo in a few hot words, for as Woislaw, unperceived by either, advanced under the shadow of the wall, Azzo said gloomily: "Leave me, foolish boy—leave me; for by that sun"—and he pointed to the full moon above them—"you will see those rays no more if you linger another moment on my path."

"And I tell you, wretch, that you either give me satisfaction for your repeated insolence, or you die," cried Franz, drawing his sword.

Azzo stretched forth his hand, and grasping the sword in the middle, it snapped like a broken reed. "I warn you for the last time," he said in a voice of thunder, as he threw the pieces into the moat. "Now, away—away, boy, from my path, or, by those below us, you are lost!"

"You or I! you or I!" cried Franz madly, as he made a rush at the sword of his antagonist, and strove to draw it from his side.

Azzo replied not; only a bitter laugh half escaped from his lips; then seizing Franz by the chest, he lifted him up like an infant, and was in the act of throwing him over the bridge, when Woislaw stepped to his side. With a grasp of his wonderful hand, into the springs of which he threw all his strength, he seized Azzo's arm, pulled it down, and obliged him to drop his victim. Azzo seemed in the highest degree astonished. Without concerning himself further about Franz, he gazed in amazement on Woislaw.

"Who are thou who darest to rob me of my prey?" he asked hesitatingly. "Is it possible? Can you be—"

"Ask not, thou bloody one! Go, seek thy nourishment! Soon comes thy hour!" replied Woislaw in a calm but firm tone.

"Ha, now I know!" cried Azzo eagerly. "Welcome, blood-brother! I give up to you this worm, and for your sake will not crush him. Farewell; our paths will soon meet again."

"Soon, very soon; farewell!" cried Woislaw, drawing Franz towards him. Azzo rushed away, and disappeared.

Franz had remained for some moments in a state of stupefaction, but suddenly started as from a dream. "I am dishonoured, dishonoured for ever!" he cried, as he pressed his clenched hands to his forehead.

"Calm yourself; you could not have conquered," said Woislaw.

"But I will conquer, or perish!" cried Franz incensed. "I will seek this adventurer in his den, and he or I must fall."

"You could not hurt him," said Woislaw. "You would infallibly be the victim."

"Then show me a way to bring the wretch to judgment," cried Franz, seizing Woislaw's hands, while tears of anger sprang to his eyes. "Disgraced as I am, I cannot live."

"You shall be revenged, and that within twenty-four hours, I hope; but only on two conditions—"

"I agree to them! I will do anything—" began the young man eagerly.

"The first is, that you do nothing, but leave everything in my hands," interrupted Woislaw. "The second, that you will assist me in persuading Franziska to do what I shall represent to her as absolutely necessary. That young lady's life is in more danger from Azzo than your own!"

"How? What?" cried Franz fiercely. "Franziska's life in danger! and from that man? Tell me, Woislaw, who is this fiend?"

"Not a word will I tell either the young lady or you, until the danger is passed," said Woislaw firmly. "The smallest indiscretion would ruin everything. No one can act here but Franziska herself, and if she refuses to do so she is irretrievably lost."

"Speak, and I will help you. I will do all you wish, but I must know—"

"Nothing, absolutely nothing," replied Woislaw. "I must have both you and Franziska yield to me unconditionally. Come now, come to her. You are to be mute on what has passed, and use every effort to induce her to accede to my proposal."

Woislaw spoke firmly, and it was impossible for Franz to make any further objection; in a few moments they both entered the hall, where they found the young girls still anxiously awaiting them.

"Oh, I have been so frightened," said Franziska, even paler than usual, as she held out her hand to Franz. "I trust all has ended peaceably."

"Everything is arranged; a couple of words were sufficient to settle the whole affair," said Woislaw cheerfully.

"But Master Franz was less concerned in it than yourself, fair lady."

"I! How do you mean? " said Franziska in surprise.

"I allude to your illness," replied the other.

"And you spoke of that to Azzo? Does he, then, know a remedy which he could not tell me himself?" she inquired, smiling painfully.

"The knight Azzo must take part in your cure; but speak to you about it he cannot, unless the remedy is to lose all its efficacy," replied Woislaw quietly.

"So it is some secret elixir, as the learned doctors say, who have so long attended me, and through whose means I only grow worse," said Franziska mournfully.

"It is certainly a secret, but is as certainly a cure," replied Woislaw.

"So said all, but none has succeeded," said the young lady peevishly.

"You might at least try it," began Bertha.

"Because your friend proposes it," said the other smiling. "I have no doubt that you, with nothing ailing you, would take all manner of drugs to please your knight; but with me the inducement is wanting, and therefore also the faith."

"I did not speak of any medicine," said Woislaw.

"Oh! a magical remedy! I am to be cured—what was it the quack who was here the other day called it?—'by sympathy.' Yes, that was it."

"I do not object to your calling it so, if you like," said Woislaw smiling; "but you must know, dear lady, that the measures I shall propose must be attended to literally, and according to the strictest directions."

"And you trust this to me?" asked Franziska.

"Certainly," said Woislaw hesitating; "but—"

"Well, why do you not proceed? Can you think that I shall fail in courage?" she asked.

"Courage is certainly necessary for the success of my plan," said Woislaw gravely; "and it is because I give you credit for a large share of that virtue, I venture to propose it at all, although for the real harmlessness of the remedy I will answer with my life, provided you follow my directions exactly."

"Well, tell me the plan, and then I can decide," said the young lady.

"I can only tell you that when we commence our operations," replied Woislaw.

"Do you think I am a child to be sent here, there, and everywhere, without a reason?" asked Franziska, with something of her old pettishness.

"You did me great injustice, dear lady, if you thought for a moment I would propose anything disagreeable to you, unless demanded by the sternest necessity," said Woislaw; "and yet I can only repeat my former words."

"Then I will not do it," cried Franziska. "I have already tried so much, and all ineffectually."

"I give you my honour as a knight, that your cure is certain, but—you must pledge yourself solemnly and unconditionally to do implicitly what I shall direct," said Woislaw earnestly.

"Oh, I implore you to consent, Franziska. Our friend would not propose anything unnecessary," said Bertha, taking both her cousin's hands.

"And let me join my entreaties to Bertha's," said Franz.

"How strange you all are!" exclaimed Franziska, shaking her head; "you make such a secret of that which I must know if I am to accomplish it, and then you declare so positively that I shall recover, when my own feelings tell me it is quite hopeless."

"I repeat, that I will answer for the result," said Woislaw, "on the condition I mentioned before, and that you have courage to carry out what you commence."

"Ha! now I understand; this, after all, is the only thing which appears doubtful to you," cried Franziska. "Well, to show you that our sex are neither wanting in the will nor in the power to accomplish deeds of daring, I give my consent."

With the last words, she offered Woislaw her hand.

"Our compact is thus sealed," she pursued smiling. "Now say, Sir Knight, how am I to commence this mysterious cure?"

"It commenced when you gave your consent," said Woislaw gravely. "Now, I have only to request that you will ask no more questions, but hold yourself in readiness to take a ride with me tomorrow an hour before sunset. I also request that you will not mention to your father a word of what has passed."

"Strange!" said Franziska.

"You have made the compact; you are not wanting in resolution; and I will answer for everything else," said Woislaw encouragingly.

"Well, so let it be. I will follow your directions," said the lady, although she still looked incredulous.

"On our return you shall know everything; before that, it is quite impossible," said Woislaw in conclusion. "Now go, dear lady, and take some rest; you will need strength for to-morrow."

It was on the morning of the following day, the sun had not

risen above an hour, and the dew still lay like a veil of pearls on the grass, or dripped from the petals of the flowers, swaying in the early breeze, when the knight Woislaw hastened over the fields towards the forest, and turned into a gloomy path, which by the direction, one could perceive, led towards the towers of Klatka. When he arrived at the old oak-tree we have before had occasion to mention, he sought carefully along the road for traces of human footsteps, but only a deer had passed that way; and seemingly satisfied with his search, he proceeded on his way, though not before he had half drawn his dagger from its sheath, as though to assure himself that it was ready for service in time of need.

Slowly he ascended the path; it was evident he carried something beneath his cloak. Arrived in the court, he left the ruins of the castle to the left, and entered the old chapel. In the chancel, he looked eagerly and earnestly around. A deathlike stillness reigned in the deserted sanctuary, only broken by the whispering of the wind in an old thorn-tree which grew outside. Woislaw had looked round him ere he perceived the door leading down to the vault; he hurried towards it, and descended. The sun's position enabled its rays to penetrate the crevices, and made the subterranean chamber so light, that one could read easily the inscriptions at the head and feet of the coffins. The knight first laid on the ground the packet he had hitherto carried under his cloak, and then going from coffin to coffin, at last remained stationary before the oldest of them. He read the inscription carefully, drew his dagger thoughtfully from its case, and endeavoured to raise the lid with its point. This was no difficult matter, for the rusty iron nails kept but a slight hold of the rotten wood. On looking in, only a heap of ashes, some remnants of dress, and a skull were the contents. He quickly closed it again, and went on to the next, passing over those of a woman and two children. Here things had much the same appearance, except that the corpse held together till the lid was raised, and then fell into dust, a few linen rags and bones being alone perceptible In the third, fourth, and nearly the next half-dozen, the bodies were in better preservation: in some, they looked a sort of yellow brown mummy; whilst in others, a skinless skull covered with hair grinned from the coverings of velvet, silk, or mildewed embroideries; all, however, were touched with the loathsome marks of decay. Only one more coffin now remained to be inspected; Woislaw approached it, and read the inscription. It was the same that had before attracted the Knight of Fahnenberg: Ezzelin von Klatka, the last possessor of the tower, was described as lying therein. Woislaw found it more difficult to raise the lid here; and it was only by the exertion of much strength he at length succeeded in extracting the nails. He did all, however, as quietly as if afraid of rousing some sleeper within; he then raised the cover, and cast a glance on the corpse. An involuntary "Ha!" burst from his lips as he stepped back a pace. If he had less expected the sight that met his eyes, he would have been far more overcome. In the coffin lay Azzo as he lived and breathed, and as Woislaw had seen him at the supper-table only the evening before. His appearance, dress and all were the same; besides, he had more the semblance of sleep than of death—no trace of decay was visible—there was even a rosy tint on his cheeks. Only the circumstance that the breast did not heave, distinguished him from one who slept. For a few moments Woislaw did not move; he could only stare into the coffin. With a hastiness in his movements not usual with him, he suddenly seized the lid, which had fallen from his hands, and laying it on the coffin, knocked the nails into their places. As soon as he had completed this work, he fetched the packet he had left at the entrance, and laying it on the top of the coffin, hastily ascended the steps, and quitted the church and the ruins.

The day passed. Before evening, Franziska requested her father to allow her to take a ride with Woislaw, under pretence of showing him the country. He, only too happy to think this a sign of amendment in his daughter, readily gave his consent; so followed by a single servant, they mounted and left the castle. Woislaw was unusually silent and serious. When Franziska began to rally him about his gravity, and the approaching sympathetic care, he replied that what was before her was no laughing matter; and that although the result would be certainly a cure, still it would leave an impression on her whole future life. In such discourse they reached the wood, and at length the oak, where they left their horses. Woislaw gave Franziska his arm, and they ascended the hill slowly and silently. They had just reached one of the half-dilapidated outworks where they could catch a glimpse of the open country, when Woislaw, speaking more to himself than to his companion, said: "In a quarter of an hour, the sun will set, and in another hour the moon will have risen; then all must be accomplished. It will soon be time to commence the work."

"Then, I should think it was time to entrust me with some idea of what it is," said Franziska, looking at him.

"Well, lady," he replied, turning towards her, and his voice was very solemn, "I entreat you, Franziska von Fahnenberg, for your own good, and as you love the father who clings to you with his whole soul, that you will weigh well my words, and that you will not interrupt me with questions which I cannot answer until the work is completed. Your life is in the greatest danger from the illness under which you are labouring; indeed, you are irrecoverably lost if you do not fully carry out what I shall now impart to you. Now, promise me to do implicitly as I shall tell you; I pledge you my knightly word it is nothing against Heaven, or the honour of your house; and, besides, it is the sole means for saving you." With these words, he held out his right hand to his companion, while he raised the other to heaven in confirmation of his oath.

"I promise you," said Franziska, visibly moved by Woislaw's solemn tone, as she laid her little white and wasted hand in his.

"Then, come; it is time," was his reply, as he led her towards the church. The last rays of the sun were just pouring through the broken windows. They entered the chancel, the best preserved part of the whole building; here there were still some old kneeling-stools, placed before the high-altar, although nothing remained of that but the stonework and a few steps; the pictures and decorations had all vanished.

"Say an Ave; you will have need of it," said Woislaw, as he himself fell on his knees.

Franziska knelt beside him, and repeated a short prayer. After a few moments, both rose. "The moment has arrived! The sun sinks, and before the moon rises, all must be over," said Woislaw quickly.

"What am I to do?" asked Franziska cheerfully.

"You see there that open vault!" replied the knight Woislaw, pointing to the door and flight of steps: "You must descend. You must go alone; I may not accompany you. When you have reached the vault you will find, close to the entrance, a coffin, on which is placed a small packet. Open this packet, and you will find three long iron nails and a hammer. Then pause for a moment; but when I begin to repeat the Credo in a loud voice, knock with all your might, first one nail, then a second, and then a third, into the lid of the coffin, right up to their heads."

Franziska stood thunderstruck; her whole body trembled, and she could not utter a word. Woislaw perceived it.

"Take courage, dear lady!" said he. "Think that you are in the hands of Heaven, and that without the will of your Creator, not a hair can fall from your head. Besides, I repeat, there is no danger."

"Well, then, I will do it," cried Franziska, in some measure regaining courage.

"Whatever you may hear, whatever takes place inside the coffin," continued Woislaw, "must have no effect upon you. Drive the nails well in, without flinching: your work must be finished before my prayer comes to an end."

Franziska shuddered, but again recovered herself. "I will do it; Heaven will send me strength," she murmured softly.

"There is one thing more," said Woislaw hesitatingly; "perhaps it is the hardest of all I have proposed, but without it your cure will not be complete. When you have done as I have told you, a sort of"—he hesitated—"a sort of liquid will flow from the coffin; in this dip your finger, and besmear the scratch on your throat."

"Horrible!" cried Franziska. "This liquid is blood. A human being lies in the coffin."

"An unearthly one lies therein! That blood is your own, but it flows in other veins," said Woislaw gloomily. "Ask no more; the sand is running out."

Franziska summoned up all her powers of mind and body, went

towards the steps which led to the vault, and Woislaw sank on his knees before the altar in quiet prayer. When the lady had descended, she found herself before the coffin on which lay the packet before mentioned. A sort of twilight reigned in the vault, and everything around was so still and peaceful, that she felt more calm, and going up to the coffin, opened the packet. She had hardly seen that a hammer and three long nails were its contents when suddenly Woislaw's voice rang through the church, and broke the stillness of the aisles. Franziska started, but recognized the appointed prayer. She seized one of the nails, and with one stroke of the hammer drove it at least an inch into the cover. All was still; nothing was heard but the echo of the stroke. Taking heart, the maiden grasped the hammer with both hands, and struck the nail twice with all her might, right up to the head into the wood. At this moment commenced a rustling noise; it seemed as though something in the interior began to move and to struggle. Franziska drew back in alarm. She was already on the point of throwing away the hammer, and flying up the steps, when Woislaw raised his voice so powerfully, and it sounded so entreatingly, that in a sort of excitement, such as would induce one to rush into a lion's den, she returned to the coffin, determined to bring things to a conclusion. Hardly knowing what she did, she placed a second nail in the centre of the lid, and after some strokes, this was likewise buried to its head. The struggle now increased fearfully, as if some living creature were striving to burst the coffin. This was so shaken by it, that it cracked and split on all sides. Half distracted, Franziska seized the third nail; she thought no more of her ailments, she only knew herself to be in terrible danger, of what kind she could not guess: in an agony that threatened to rob her of her senses, and in the midst of the turning and cracking of the coffin, in which low groans were now heard, she struck the third nail in equally tight. At this moment, she began to lose consciousness. She wished to hasten away, but staggered; and mechanically grasping at something to save herself by, she seized the corner of the coffin, and sank fainting beside it on the ground.

A quarter of an hour might have elapsed, when she again

opened her eyes. She looked around her. Above was the starry sky, and the moon, which shed her cold light on the ruins and on the tops of the old oak-trees. Franziska was lying outside the church walls, Woislaw on his knees beside her, holding her hand in his.

"Heaven be praised that you live!" he cried, with a sigh of relief. "I was beginning to doubt whether the remedy had not been too severe, and yet it was the only thing to save you."

Franziska recovered her full consciousness very gradually. The past seemed to her like a dreadful dream. Only a few moments before, that fearful scene; and now this quiet all around her. She hardly dared at first to raise her eyes, and shuddered when she found herself only a few paces removed from the spot where she had undergone such terrible agony. She listened half unconsciously, now to the pacifying words Woislaw addressed to her, now to the whistling of the servant, who stood by the horses, and who, to while away his time, was imitating the evening-song of a belated cow-herd.

"Let us go," whispered Franziska, as she strove to raise herself "But what is this? My shoulder is wet, my throat, my hand—"

"It is probably the evening dew on the grass," said Woislaw gently.

"No; it is blood!" she cried, springing up with horror in her tone. "See, my hand is full of blood!"

"Oh, you are mistaken—surely mistaken," said Woislaw stammering. "Or perhaps the wound on your neck may have opened! Pray, feel whether this is the case." He seized her hand, and directed it to the spot.

"I do not perceive anything; I feel no pain," she said at length, somewhat angrily.

"Then, perhaps, when you fainted, you may have struck a corner of the coffin, or have torn yourself with the point of one of the nails," suggested Woislaw.

"Oh, of what do you remind me!" cried Franziska shuddering. "Let us away—away! I entreat you, come! I will not remain a moment longer near this dreadful, dreadful place."

They descended the path much quicker than they came. Woislaw placed his companion on her horse, and they were soon on their way home.

When they approached the castle, Franziska began to inundate her protector with questions about the preceding adventure; but he declared that her present state of excitement must make him defer all explanations till the morning, when her curiosity should be satisfied. On their arrival, he conducted her at once to her room, and told the knight his daughter was too much fatigued with her ride to appear at the supper-table. On the following morning, Franziska rose earlier than she had done for a long time. She assured her friend it was the first time since her illness commenced that she had been really refreshed by her sleep, and, what was still more remarkable, she had not been troubled by her old terrible dream. Her improved looks were not only remarked Bertha, but by Franz and the knight; and with Woislaw's permission, she related the adventures of the previous evening. No sooner had she concluded, than Woislaw was completely stormed with questions about such a strange occurrence.

"Have you" said the latter, turning towards his host, "ever heard of Vampires?"

"Often," replied he; "but I have never believed in them."

"Nor did I," said Woislaw; "but I have been assured of their existence by experience."

"Oh, tell us what occurred," cried Bertha eagerly, as a light seemed to dawn on her.

"It was during my first campaign in Hungary," began Woislaw, "when I was rendered helpless for some time by this sword-cut of a janizary across my face, and another on my shoulder. I had been taken into the house of a respectable family in a small town. It consisted of the father and mother, and a daughter about twenty years of age. They obtained their living by selling the very good wine of the country, and the taproom was always full of visitors. Although the family were well to do in the world, there seemed to brood over them a continual melancholy, caused by the constant illness of the only daughter, a very pretty and excellent girl. She had always bloomed like a rose, but for some months she had been getting so thin and wasted, and that without any satisfactory reason: they tried every means to restore her, but in vain. As the army had encamped quite in the neighbourhood, of course a number of people of all countries assembled in the tavern. Amongst these there was one man who came every evening, when the moon shone, who struck everybody by the peculiarity of his manners and appearance; he looked dried up and deathlike, and hardly spoke at all; but what he did say was bitter and sarcastic. Most attention was excited towards him by the circumstance, that although he always ordered a cup of the best wine, and now and then raised it to his lips, the cup was always as full after his departure as at first."

"This all agrees wonderfully with the appearance of Azzo," said Bertha, deeply interested.

"The daughter of the house," continued Woislaw, "became daily worse, despite the aid not only of Christian doctors, but of many amongst the heathen prisoners, who were consulted in the hope that they might have some magical remedy to propose. It was singular that the girl always complained of a dream, in which the unknown guest worried and plagued her."

"Just the same as your dream, Franziska," cried Bertha.

"One evening," resumed Woislaw, "an old Sclavonian—who had made many voyages to Turkey and Greece, and had even seen the New World—and I were sitting over our wine, and sat down at the table. The bottle passed quickly between my friend and me, whilst we talked of all manner of things, of our adventures, and of passages in our lives, both horrible and amusing. We went on chatting thus for about an hour, and drank a tolerable quantity of wine. The unknown had remained perfectly silent the whole time, only smiling contemptuously every now and then. He now paid his money, and was going away. All this had quietly worried me—perhaps the wine had got a little into my head—so I said to the stranger: 'Hold, you stony stranger; you have hitherto done nothing but listen, and have not even emptied your cup. Now you shall take your turn in telling us something amusing, and if you do not drink up your wine, it shall produce a quarrel between us.' 'Yes,' said the Sclavonian, 'you must remain; you shall chat and drink, too;' and he grasped—for although no longer young, he was big and very strong—the stranger by the shoulder, to pull him down to his seat again: the latter, however, although as thin as a skeleton, with one movement of his hand flung the Sclavonian to the middle of the room, and half stunned him for a moment. I now approached to hold the stranger back. I caught him by the arm; and although the springs of my iron hand were less powerful than those I have at present, I must have gripped him rather hard in my anger, for after looking grimly at me for a moment, he bent towards me and whispered in my ear: 'Let me go from the gripe of your fist, I see you are my brother, therefore do not hinder me from seeking my bloody nourishment. I am hungry!' Surprised by such words, I let him loose, and almost before I was aware he had left the room. As soon as I had in some degree recovered from my astonishment, I told the Sclavonian what I had heard. He started, evidently alarmed. I asked him to tell me the cause of his fears, and pressed him for an explanation of those extraordinary words. On our way to his lodging, he complied with my request. 'The stranger,' said he, 'is a Vampire!'"

"How?" cried the knight, Franziska, and Bertha simultaneously, in a voice of horror. "So this Azzo was —"

"Nothing less. He also was a Vampire!" replied Woislaw. "But at all events his hellish thirst is quenched for ever; he will never return.—But I have not finished. As in my country vampires had never been heard of, I questioned the Sclavonian minutely. He said that in Hungary, Croatia, Dalmatia, and Bosnia, these hellish guests were not uncommon. They were deceased persons, who had either once served as nourishment to vampires, or who had died in deadly sin, or under excommunication; and that whenever the moon shone, they rose from their graves, and sucked the blood of the living."

"Horrible! " cried Franziska. "If you had told me all this beforehand, I should never have accomplished the work."

"So I thought; and yet it must be executed by the sufferers themselves, while some one else performs the devotions," replied Woislaw. "The Sclavonian," he continued after a short pause, "added many other facts with regard to these unearthly visitants. He said that whilst their victim wasted, they themselves improved in appearance, and that a vampire possessed enormous strength—"

"Now I can understand the change your false hand produced on Azzo," interrupted Franz.

"Yes, that was it," replied Woislaw. "Azzo, as well as the other vampire, mistook its great power for that of a natural one, and concluded I was one of his own species.—You may now imagine, dear lady," he continued, turning to Franziska, "how alarmed I was at your appearance when I arrived: all you and Bertha told me increased my anxiety; and when I saw Azzo, I could doubt no longer that he was a vampire. As I learned from your account that a grave with the name Ezzelin von Klatka lay in the neighbourhood, I had no doubt that you might be saved if I could only induce you to assist me. It did not appear to me advisable to impart the whole facts of the case, for your bodily powers were so impaired, that an idea of the horrors before you might have quite unfitted you for the exertion; for this reason, I arranged everything in the manner in which it has taken place."

"You did wisely," replied Franziska shuddering. "I can never be grateful enough to you. Had I known what was required of me, I never could have undertaken the deed."

"That was what I feared," said Woislaw; "but fortune has favoured us all through."

"And what became of the unfortunate girl in Hungary?" inquired Bertha.

"I know not," replied Woislaw. "That very evening there was an alarm of Turks, and we were ordered off. I never heard anything more of her."

The conversation upon these strange occurrences continued for some time longer. The knight determined to have the vault at Klatka walled up for ever. This took place on the following day; the knight alleging as a reason that he did not wish the dead to be disturbed by irreverent hands.

Franziska recovered gradually. Her health had been so severely shaken, that it was long ere her strength was so much restored as to allow of her being considered out of danger. The young lady's character underwent a great change in the interval. Its former strength was, perhaps, in some degree diminished, but in place of that, she had acquired a benevolent softness, which brought out all her best qualities. Franz continued his attentions to his cousin; but, perhaps, owing to a hint from Bertha, he was less assiduous in his exhibition of them. His inclinations did not lead him to the battle, the camp, or the attainment of honours; his great aim was to increase the good condition and happiness of his tenants, and to this he contributed the whole energy of his mind. Franziska could not withstand the unobtrusive signs of the young man's continued attachment; and it was not long ere the credit she was obliged to yield to his noble efforts for the welfare of his fellow-creatures, changed into a liking, which went on increasing, until at length it assumed the character of love. As Woislaw insisted on making Bertha his wife before he returned to Silesia, it was arranged that the marriage should take place at their present abode. How joyful was the surprise of the knight of Fahnenberg, when his daughter and Franz likewise entreated his blessing, and expressed their desire of being united on the same day! That day soon came round, and it saw the bright looks of two happy couples.

The Last Lords of Gardonal

by William Gilbert

Part I

One of the most picturesque objects of the valley of the Engadin is the ruined castle of Gardonal, near the village of Madaline. In the feudal times it was the seat of a family of barons, who possessed as their patrimony the whole of the valley, which with the castle had descended from father to son for many generations. The two last of the race were brothers; handsome, well-made, fine-looking young men, but in nature they more resembled fiends than human beings—so cruel, rapacious, and tyrannical were they. During the earlier part of his life their father had been careful of his patrimony. He had also been unusually just to the serfs on his estates, and in consequence they had attained to such a condition of comfort and prosperity as was rarely met with among those in the power of the feudal lords of the country; most of whom were arbitrary and exacting in the extreme. For several years in the latter part of his life he had been subject to a severe illness, which had confined him to the castle, and the management of his possessions and the government of his serfs had thus fallen into the hands of his sons. Although the old baron had placed so much power in their hands; still he was far from resigning his own authority. He exacted a strict account from them of the manner in which they performed the different duties he had intrusted to them; and having a strong suspicion of their character, and the probability of their endeavouring to conceal their misdoings, he caused agents to watch them secretly, and to report to him as to the correctness of the statements they gave. These agents possibly knowing that the old man had but a short time to live invariably gave a most favourable description of the conduct of the two young nobles, which, it must be admitted, was not, during their father's lifetime, particularly reprehensible on the whole. Still, they frequently showed as much of the cloven foot as to prove to the tenants what they had to expect at no distant day.

At the old baron's death, Conrad, the elder, inherited as his por-tion the castle of Gardonal, and the whole valley of Engadin; while to Hermann, the younger, was assigned some immense estates belong to his father in the Bresciano district; for even in those early days, there was considerable intercourse between the inhabitants of that northern portion of Italy and those of the valley of the Engadin. The old baron had also willed, that should either of his sons die without children his estates should go to the survivor.

Conrad accordingly now took possession of the castle and its territory, and Hermann of the estates on the southern side of the Alps which, although much smaller than those left to his elder brother, were still of great value. Notwithstanding the disparity in the worth of the legacies bequeathed to the two brothers, a per-fectly good feeling existed between them, which promised to con-tinue, their tastes being the same, while the mountains which divided them tended to the continuance of peace.

Conrad had hardly been one single week feudal lord of the Engadin before the inhabitants found, to their sorrow, how great was the difference between him and the old baron. Instead of the score of armed retainers his father had kept, Conrad increased the number to three hundred men, none of whom were natives of the valley. They had been chosen with great care from a body of

Bohemian, German, and Italian outlaws, who at that time infested the borders of the Grisons, or had found refuge in the fastnesses of the mountains—men capable of any atrocity and to whom pity was unknown. From these miscreants the baron especially chose for his body-guard those who were ignorant of the language spoken by the peasantry of the Engadin, as they would be less likely to be influenced by any supplications or excuses which might be made to them when in the performance of their duty. Although the keeping of so numerous a body of armed retainers might naturally be considered to have entailed great expense, such a conclusion would be most erroneous, at least as far as regarded the present baron, who was as avaricious as he was despotic. He contrived to support his soldiers by imposing a most onerous tax on his tenants, irrespective of his ordinary feudal imposts; and woe to the unfortunate villagers who from inability, or from a sense of the injustice inflicted on them, did not contribute to the uttermost farthing the amount levied on them. In such a case a party of soldiers was immediately sent off to the defaulting village to collect the tax, with permission to live at free quarters till the money was paid; and they knew their duty too well to return home till they had succeeded in their errand. In doing this they were frequently merciless in the extreme, exacting the money by torture or any other means they pleased; and when they had been successful in obtaining the baron's dues, by way of further punishment they generally robbed the poor peasantry of everything they had which was worth the trouble of carrying away, and not unfrequently, from a spirit of sheer mischief, they spoiled all that remained. Many were the complaints which reached the ears of the baron of the cruel behaviour of his retainers; but in no case did they receive any redress; the baron making it a portion of his policy that no crimes committed by those under his command should be investigated, so long as those crimes took place when employed in collecting taxes which he had imposed, and which had remained unpaid.

But the depredations and cruelties of the Baron Conrad were not confined solely to the valley of the Engadin. Frequently in the summer-time when the snows had melted on the mountains, so as to make the road practicable for his soldiers and their plunder, he would make a raid on the Italian side of the Alps. There they would rob and commit every sort of atrocity with impunity; and when they had collected sufficient booty they returned with it to the castle. Loud indeed were the complaints which reached the authorities of Milan. With routine tardiness, the government never took any energetic steps to punish the offenders until the winter had set in; and to cross the mountains in that season would have been almost an impossibility, at all events for an army. When the spring returned, more prudential reasons prevailed, and the matter, gradually diminishing in interest, was at last allowed to die out without any active measures being taken. Again, the districts in which the atrocities had been committed were hardly looked upon by the Milanese government as being Italian. The people themselves were beginning to be infected by a heresy which approached closely to the Protestantism of the present day; nor was their language that of Italy, but a patois of their own. Thus the government began to consider it unadvisable to attempt to punish the baron, richly as he deserved it, on behalf of those who after all were little worthy of the protection they demanded. The only real step they took to chastise him was to get him excommunicated by the Pope; which, as the baron and his followers professed no religion at all, was treated by them with ridicule.

It happened that in one of his marauding expeditions in the Valteline the baron, when near Bormio, saw a young girl of extraordinary beauty. He was only attended at the time by two followers, else it is more than probable he would have made her a prisoner and carried her off to Gardonal. As it was he would probably have made the attempt had she not been surrounded by a number of peasants, who were working in some fields belonging to her father. The baron was also aware that the militia of the town, who had been expecting his visit, were under arms, and on an alarm being given could be on the spot in a few minutes. Now as the baron combined with his despotism a considerable amount of cunning, he merely attempted to enter into conversation with the girl. Finding his advances coldly received, he contented himself with inquiring of one of the peasants the girl's name and place of abode. He received for reply that her name was Teresa Biffi, and that she was the daughter of a substantial farmer, who with his wife and four children (of whom Teresa was the eldest) lived in a house at the extremity of the land he occupied.

As soon as the baron had received this information, he left the spot and proceeded to the farmer's house, which he inspected externally with great care. He found it was of considerable size, strongly built of stone, with iron bars to the lower windows, and a strong well-made oaken door which could be securely fastened from the inside. After having made the round of the house (which he did alone), he returned to his two men, whom, in order to avoid suspicion, he had placed at a short distance from the building, in a spot where they could not easily be seen.

"Ludovico," he said to one of them who was his lieutenant and invariably accompanied him in all his expeditions, "mark well that house; for some day, or more probably night, you may have to pay it a visit."

Ludovico merely said in reply that he would be always ready and willing to perform any order his master might honour him with, and the baron, with his men, then left the spot.

The hold the beauty of Teresa Biffi had taken upon the imagination of the baron actually looked like enchantment. His love for her, instead of diminishing by time, seemed to increase daily. At last he resolved on making her his wife; and about a month after he had seen her, he commissioned his lieutenant Ludovico to carry to Biffi an offer of marriage with his daughter; not dreaming, at the moment, of the possibility of a refusal. Ludovico immediately started on his mission and in due time arrived at the farmer's house and delivered the baron's message. To Ludovico's intense surprise, however, he received from Biffi a positive refusal. Not daring to take back so uncourteous a reply to his master, Ludovico went on to describe the great advantage which would accrue to the farmer and his family if the baron's proposal were accepted. Not only, he said, would Teresa be a lady of the highest rank, and in possession of enormous wealth both in gold and jewels, but that the other members of her family would also be ennobled, and each of them, as they grew up, would receive appointments under the baron, besides having large estates allotted to them in the Engadin Valley.

The farmer listened with patience to Ludovico, and when he had concluded, he replied—

"Tell your master I have received his message, and that I am ready to admit that great personal advantages might accrue to me and my family by accepting his offer. Say, that although I am neither noble nor rich, that yet at the same time I am not poor; but were I as poor as the blind mendicant whom you passed on the road in coming hither, I would spurn such an offer from so infamous a wretch as the baron. You say truly that he is well known for his power and his wealth; but the latter has been obtained by robbing both rich and poor, who had not the means to resist him, and his power has been greatly strengthened by engaging in his service a numerous band of robbers and cut-throats, who are ready and willing to murder any one at his bidding. You have my answer, and the sooner you quit this neighbourhood the better, for I can assure you that any one known to be in the service of the Baron Conrad is likely to meet with a most unfavourable reception from those who live around us."

"Then you positively refuse his offer?" said Ludovico.

"Positively, and without the slightest reservation," was the farmer's reply.

"And you wish me to give him the message in the terms you have made use of?"

"Without omitting a word," was the farmer's reply. "At the same time, you may add to it as many of the same description as you please."

"Take care," said Ludovico. "There is yet time for you to reconsider your decision. If you insist on my taking your message to the baron, I must of course do so; but in that case make your peace with heaven as soon as you can, for the baron is not a man to let such an insult pass. Follow my advice, and accept his offer ere it is too late."

"I have no other answer to give you," said Biffi.

"I am sorry for it," said Ludovico, heaving a deep sigh; "I have now no alternative," and mounting his horse he rode away.

Now it must not be imagined that the advice Ludovico gave the farmer, and the urgent requests and arguments he offered, were altogether the genuine effusions of his heart. On the contrary, Ludovico had easily perceived, on hearing the farmer's first refusal, that there was no chance of the proposal being accepted. He had therefore occupied his time during the remaining portion of the interview in carefully examining the premises, and mentally taking note of the manner in which they could be most easily entered, as he judged rightly enough, that before long he might be sent to the house on a far less peaceable mission.

Nothing could exceed the rage of the baron when he heard the farmer's message.

"You cowardly villain!" he said to Ludovico, "did you allow the wretch to live who could send such a message to your master?"

"So please you," said Ludovico. "What could I do?"

"You could have struck him to the heart with your dagger, could you not?" said the baron. "I have known you do such a thing to an old woman for half the provocation. Had it been Biffi's wife instead you might have shown more courage."

"Had I followed my own inclination," said Ludovico, "I would have killed the fellow on the spot; but then I could not have brought away the young lady with me, for there were too many persons about the house and in the fields at the time. So I thought, before acting further, I had better let you hear his answer. One favour I hope your excellency will grant me, that if the fellow is to be punished you will allow me to inflict it as a reward for the skill I showed in keeping my temper when I heard the message."

"Perhaps you have acted wisely, Ludovico," said the baron, after a few moments' silence. "At present my mind is too much ruffled by the villain's impertinence to think calmly on the subject. Tomorrow we will speak of it again."

Next day the baron sent for his lieutenant, and said to him—

"Ludovico, I have now a commission for you to execute which I think will be exactly to your taste. Take with you six men whom you can trust, and start this afternoon for Bormio. Sleep at some village on the road, but let not one word escape you as to your errand. Tomorrow morning leave the village—but separately—so that you may not be seen together, as it is better to avoid suspicion. Meet again near the farmer's house, and arrive there, if possible, before evening has set in, for in all probability you will have to make an attack upon the house, and you may thus become well acquainted with the locality before doing so; but keep yourselves concealed, otherwise you will spoil all. After you have done this, retire some distance, and remain concealed till midnight, as then all the family will be in their first sleep, and you will experience less difficulty than if you began later. I particularly wish you to enter the house without using force, but if you cannot do so, break into it in any way you consider best. Bring out the girl and do her no harm. If any resistance is made by her father, kill him; but not unless you are compelled, as I do not wish to enrage his daughter against me. However, let nothing prevent you from securing her. Burn the house down or anything you please, but bring her here. If you execute your mission promptly and to my satisfaction, I promise you and those with you a most liberal reward. Now go and get ready to depart as speedily as you can."

Ludovico promised to execute the baron's mission to the letter, and shortly afterwards left the castle accompanied by six of the greatest ruffians he could find among the men-at-arms.

Although on the spur of the moment Biffi had sent so defiant a message to the baron, he afterwards felt considerable uneasiness as to the manner in which it would be received. He did not repent having refused the proposal, but he knew that the baron was a man of the most cruel and vindictive disposition, and would in all probability seek some means to be avenged. The only defence he could adopt was to make the fastenings of his house as secure as possible, and to keep at least one of his labourers about him whom he could send as a messenger to Bormio for assistance, and to arouse the inhabitants in the immediate vicinity, in case of his being attacked. Without any hesitation all promised to aid Biffi in every way in their power, for he had acquired great renown among the inhabitants of the place for the courage he had shown in refusing so indignantly the baron's offer of marriage for his daughter.

About midnight, on the day after Ludovico's departure from the castle, Biffi was aroused by some one knocking at the door of his house, and demanding admission. It was Ludovico, for after attempting in vain to enter the house secretly, he had concealed his men, determining to try the effect of treachery before using force. On the inquiry being made as to who the stranger was, he replied that he was a poor traveller who had lost his way, and begged that he might be allowed a night's lodging, as he was so weary he could not go a step further.

"I am sorry for you," said Biffi, "but I cannot allow you to enter this house before daylight. As the night is fine and warm you can easily sleep on the straw under the windows, and in the morning I will let you in and give you a good breakfast."

Again and again did Ludovico plead to be admitted, but in vain; Biffi would not be moved from his resolution. At last, however, the bravo's patience got exhausted, and suddenly changing his manner he roared out in a threatening tone, "If you don't let me in, you villain, I will burn your house over your head. I have here, as you may see, plenty of men to help me to put my threat into execution," he continued, pointing to the men, who had now come up, "so you had better let me in at once."

In a moment Biffi comprehended the character of the person he had to deal with; so, instead of returning any answer, he retired from the window and alarmed the inmates of the house. He also told the labourer whom he had engaged to sleep there to drop from a window at the back and run as fast as he could to arouse the inhabitants in the vicinity, and tell them that his house was attacked by the baron and his men. He was to beg them to arm themselves and come to his aid as quickly as possible, and having done this, he was to go on to Bormio on the same errand. The poor fellow attempted to carry out his master's orders; but in dropping from the window he fell with such force on the ground that he could only move with difficulty, and in trying to crawl away he was observed by some of the baron's men, who immediately set on him and killed him.

Ludovico, finding that he could not enter the house either secretly or by threatenings, attempted to force open the door, but it was so firmly barricaded from within that he did not succeed; while in the meantime Biffi and his family employed themselves in placing wooden faggots and heavy articles of furniture against it, thus making it stronger than ever. Ludovico, finding he could not gain an entrance by the door, told his men to look around in search of a ladder, so that they might get to the windows on the first floor, as those on the ground floor were all small, high up, and well barricaded, as was common in Italian houses of the time; but in spite of all their efforts no ladder could be found. He now deliberated what step he should next take. As it was getting late, he saw that if they did not succeed in effecting an entrance quickly the dawn would break upon them, and the labourers going to their work would raise an alarm. At last one man suggested that as abundance of fuel could be obtained from the stacks at the back of the house they might place a quantity of it against the door and set fire to it; adding that the sight of the flames would soon make the occupants glad to effect their escape by the first-floor windows.

The suggestion was no sooner made than acted upon. A quantity of dry fuel was piled up against the house door to the height of many feet, and a light having been procured by striking a flint stone against the hilt of a sword over some dried leaves, fire was set to the pile. From the dry nature of the fuel, the whole mass was in a blaze in a few moments. But the scheme did not have the effect Ludovico had anticipated. True, the family rushed towards the windows in the front of the house, but when they saw the flames rising so fiercely they retreated in the utmost alarm. Meanwhile the screams from the women and children—who had now lost all self-control—mingled with the roar of the blazing element which, besides having set fire to the faggots and furniture placed within the door, had now reached a quantity of fodder and Indian corn stored on the ground floor.

Ludovico soon perceived that the whole house was in flames, and that the case was becoming desperate. Not only was there the danger of the fire alarming the inhabitants in the vicinity by the light it shed around, but he also reflected what would be the rage of his master if the girl should perish in the flames, and the consequent punishment which would be inflicted on him and those under his command if he returned empty-handed. He now called out to Biffi and his family to throw themselves out of the window, and that he and his men would save them. It was some time before he was understood, but at last Biffi brought the two younger children to the window, and, lowering them as far as he could, he let them fall into the arms of Ludovico and his men, and they reached the ground in safety.

Biffi now returned for the others, and saw Teresa standing at a short distance behind him. He took her by the hand to bring her forward, and they had nearly reached the window, when she heard a scream from her mother, who being an incurable invalid was confined to her bed. Without a moment's hesitation, the girl turned back to assist her, and the men below, who thought that the prey they wanted was all but in their hands, and cared little about the fate of the rest of the family, were thus disappointed. Ludovico now anxiously awaited the reappearance of Teresa—but he waited in vain. The flames had gained entire mastery, and even the roof had taken fire. The screams of the inmates were now no longer heard, for if not stifled in the smoke they were lost in the roar of the fire; whilst the glare which arose from it illumined the landscape far and near.

It so happened that a peasant, who resided about a quarter of a mile from Biffi's house, had to go a long distance to his work, and having risen at an unusually early hour, he saw the flames, and aroused the inmates of the other cottages in the village, who immediately armed themselves and started off to the scene of the disaster, imagining, but too certainly, that it was the work of an incendiary. The alarm was also communicated to another village, and from thence to Bormio, and in a short time a strong band of armed men had collected, and proceeded together to assist in extinguishing the flames. On their arrival at the house, they found the place one immense heap of ashes—not a soul was to be seen, for Ludovico and his men had already decamped.

The dawn now broke, and the assembled peasantry made some attempt to account for the fire. At first they were induced to attribute it to accident, but on searching around they found the dead body of the murdered peasant, and afterwards the two children who had escaped, and who in their terror had rushed into a thick copse to conceal themselves. With great difficulty they gathered from them sufficient to show that the fire had been caused by a band of robbers who had come for the purpose of plundering the house; and their suspicion fell immediately on Baron Conrad, without any better proof than his infamous reputation.

As soon as Ludovico found that an alarm had been given, he and his men started off to find their horses, which they had hidden among some trees about a mile distant from Biffi's house. The daylight was just breaking, and objects around them began to be visible, but not so clearly as to allow them to see for any distance. Suddenly one of the men pointed to an indistinct figure in white some little way in advance of them. Ludovico halted for a moment to see what it might be, and, with his men, watched it attentively as it appeared to fly from them.

"It is the young girl herself," said one of the men. "She has escaped from the fire; and that was exactly as she appeared in her white dress with her father at the window. I saw her well, and am sure I am not mistaken."

"It is indeed the girl," said another. "I also saw her."

"I hope you are right," said Ludovico; "and if so, it will be fortunate indeed, for should we return without her we may receive but a rude reception from the baron."

They now quickened their pace, but, fast as they walked, the figure in white walked quite as rapidly. Ludovico, who of course began to suspect that it was Teresa attempting to escape from them, commanded his men to run as fast as they could in order to reach her. Although they tried their utmost, the figure, however, still kept the same distance before them. Another singularity about it was, that as daylight advanced the figure appeared to become less distinct, and ere they had reached their horses it seemed to have melted away.

Part II

Before mounting their horses, Ludovico held a consultation with his men as to what course they had better adopt; whether they should depart at once or search the neighbourhood for the girl. Both suggestions seemed to be attended with danger. If they delayed their departure, they might be attacked by the peasantry, who by this time were doubtless in hot pursuit of them; and if they returned to the baron without Teresa, they were almost certain to receive a severe punishment for failing in their enterprise. At last the idea struck Ludovico that a good round lie might possibly succeed with the baron and do something to avert his anger, while there was little hope of its in the slightest manner availing with the enraged peasantry. He therefore gave the order for his men to mount their horses, resolving to tell the baron that Teresa had escaped from the flames, and had begged their assistance, but a number of armed inhabitants of Bormio chancing to approach, she had sought their protection. A great portion of this statement could be substantiated by his men, as they still fully believed that the figure in white which they had so indistinctly seen was the girl herself. Ludovico and his men during their homeward journey had great difficulty in crossing the mountains, in consequence of a heavy fall of snow (for it was now late in the autumn). Next day they arrived at the castle of Gardonal.

It would be difficult to describe the rage of the baron when he heard that his retainers had been unsuccessful in their mission. He ordered Ludovico to be thrown into a dungeon, where he remained for more than a month, and was only then liberated in consequence of the baron needing his services for some expedition requiring special skill and courage. The other men were also punished, though less severely than their leader, on whom, of course, they laid all the blame.

For some time after Ludovico's return, the baron occupied himself in concocting schemes, not only to secure the girl Teresa (for he fully believed the account Ludovico had given of her escape), but to revenge himself on the inhabitants of Bormio for the part they had taken in the affair; and it was to carry out these schemes that he liberated Ludovico from prison.

The winter had passed, and the spring sun was rapidly melting the snows on the mountains, when one morning three travel-stained men, having the appearance of respectable burghers, arrived at the Hospice, and requested to be allowed an interview with the Innominato. A messenger was despatched to the castle, who shortly afterwards returned, saying that his master desired the visitors should immediately be admitted into his presence. When they arrived at the castle they found him fully prepared to receive them, a handsome repast being spread out for their refreshment. At first the travellers seemed under some restraint; but this was soon dispelled by the friendly courtesy of the astrologer. After partaking of the viands which had been set before them, the Innominato inquired the object of their visit. One of them who had been evidently chosen as spokesman, then rose from his chair and addressed their host as follows:

"We have been sent to your excellency by the inhabitants of Bormio as a deputation, to ask your advice and assistance in a strait we are in at present. Late in the autumn of last year, the Baron Conrad, feudal lord of the Engadin, was on some not very honest expedition in our neighbourhood, when by chance he saw a very beautiful girl, of the name of Teresa Biffi, whose father occupied a large farm about half a league from the town. The baron, it appears, became so deeply enamoured of the girl that he afterwards sent a messenger to her father with an offer of marriage for his daughter. Biffi, knowing full well the infamous reputation of the baron, unhesitatingly declined his proposal and in such indignant terms as to arouse the tyrant's anger to the highest pitch. Determining not only to possess himself of the girl, but to avenge the insult he had received, he sent a body of armed retainers, who in the night attacked the farmer's house, and endeavoured to effect an entrance by breaking open the door. Finding they could not succeed, and after murdering one of the servants who had been sent to a neighbouring village to give the alarm, they set fire to the house, and with the exception of two children who contrived to escape, the whole family, including the young girl herself, perished in the flames. It appears, however, that the baron (doubtless through his agents) received a false report that the young girl had escaped, and was taken under the protection of some of the inhabitants of Bormio. In consequence, he sent another body of armed men, who arrived in the night at the house of the podesta, and contrived to make his only son, a boy of about fifteen years old, a prisoner, bearing him off to the baron's castle. They left word, that unless Teresa Biffi was placed in their power before the first day of May, not only would the youth be put to death, but the baron would also wreak vengeance on the whole town. On the perpetration of this last atrocity, we again applied to the government of Milan for protection; but although our reception was most courteous, and we were promised assistance, we have too good reason to doubt our receiving it. Certainly up to the present time no steps have been taken in the matter, nor has a single soldier been sent, although the time named for the death of the child has nearly expired. The townsmen therefore, having heard of your great wisdom and power, your willingness to help those who are in distress, as well as to protect the weak and oppressed, have sent us to ask you to take them under your protection; as the baron is not a man to scruple at putting such a threat into execution."

The Innominato, who had listened to the delegate with great patience and attention, told him that he had no soldiers or retainers at his orders; while the baron, whose wicked life was known to him, had many.

"But your excellency has great wisdom, and from all we have heard, we feel certain that you could protect us."

"Your case," said the Innominato, "is a very sad one, I admit, and you certainly ought to be protected from the baron's machinations. I will not disguise from you that I have the power to help you. Tell the unhappy podesta that he need be under no alarm as to his son's safety, and that I will oblige the baron to release him. My art tells me that the boy is still alive, though confined in prison. As for your friends who sent you to me, tell them that the baron shall do them no harm. All you have to do is, to contrive some means by which the baron may hear that the girl Teresa Biffi has been placed by me where he will never find her without my permission."

"But Teresa Biffi," said the delegate, "perished with her father; and the baron will wreak his vengeance both on you and us, when he finds you cannot place the girl in his power."

"Fear nothing, but obey my orders," said the Innominato. "Do what I have told you, and I promise you shall have nothing to dread from him. The sooner you carry out my directions the better."

The deputation now returned to Bormio, and related all that had taken place at their interview with the Innominato. Although the result of their mission was scarcely considered satisfactory, they determined, after much consideration, to act on the astrologer's advice. But how to carry it out was a very difficult matter. This was, however, overcome by one of the chief inhabitants of the town—a man of most determined courage—offering himself as a delegate to the baron, to convey to him the Innominato's message. Without hesitation the offer was gratefully accepted, and the next day he started on his journey. No sooner had he arrived at the castle of Gardonal, and explained the object of his mission, than he was ushered into the presence of the baron, whom he found in the great hall, surrounded by a numerous body of armed men.

"Well," said the baron, as soon as the delegate had entered, "have your townspeople come to their senses at last, and sent me the girl Teresa?"

"No, they have not, baron," was the reply, "for she is not in their custody. All they can do is to inform you where you may possibly receive some information about her."

"And where may that be?"

"The only person who knows where she may be found is the celebrated astrologer who lives in a castle near Lecco."

"Ah now, you are trifling with me," said the baron sternly. "You must be a great fool or a very bold man to try such an experiment as that."

"I am neither the one nor the other, your excellency; nor am I trifling with you. What I have told you is the simple truth."

"And how did you learn it?"

"From the Innominato's own lips."

"Then you applied to him for assistance against me," said the baron, furiously.

"That is hardly correct, your excellency," said the delegate. "It is true we applied to him for advice as to the manner in which we should act in case you should attack us, and put your threat into execution respecting the son of the podesta."

"And what answer did he give you?"

"Just what I have told you—that he alone knows where Teresa Biffi is to be found, and that you could not remove her from the protection she is under without his permission."

"Did he send that message to me in defiance?" said the baron.

"I have no reason to believe so, your excellency."

The baron was silent for some time; he then inquired of the delegate how many armed retainers the Innominato kept.

"None, I believe," was the reply. "At any rate, there were none to be seen when the deputation from the town visited him."

The baron was again silent for some moments, and seemed deeply absorbed in thought. He would rather have met with any other opponent than the Innominato, whose reputation was well known to him, and whose learning he dreaded more than the power of any nobleman—no matter how many armed retainers he could bring against him.

"I very much suspect," he said at last, "that some deception is being practised on me. But should my suspicion be correct I shall exact terrible vengeance. I shall detain you," he continued, turning abruptly and fiercely on the delegate, "as a hostage while I visit the Innominato; and if I do not succeed with him, you shall die on the same scaffold as the son of your podesta."

It was in vain that the delegate protested against being detained as a prisoner, saying that it was against all rules of knightly usage; but the baron would not listen to reason, and the unfortunate man was immediately hurried out of the hall and imprisoned.

Although the baron by no means liked the idea of an interview with the Innominato, he immediately made preparations to visit him, and the day after the delegate's arrival he set out on his journey, attended by only four of his retainers. It should here be mentioned, that it is more than probable the baron would have avoided meeting the Innominato on any other occasion whatever, so great was the dislike he had to him. He seemed to be acting under some fatality; some power seemed to impel him in his endeavours to obtain Teresa which it was impossible to account for.

The road chosen by the baron to reach the castle of the Innominato was rather a circuitous one. In the first place, he did not consider it prudent to pass through the Valteline; and in the second, he thought that by visiting his brother on his way he might be able to obtain some particulars as to the character of the mysterious individual whom he was about to see, as his reputation would probably be better known among the inhabitants of the Bergamo district than by those in the valley of the Engadin.

The baron arrived safely at his brother's castle, where the reports which had hitherto indistinctly reached him of the wonderful power and skill of the astrologer were fully confirmed. After remaining a day with his brother, the baron started for Lecco. Under an assumed name he stayed here for two days, in order that he might receive the report of one of his men, whom he had sent forward to ascertain whether the Innominato had any armed men in his castle; for, being capable of any act of treachery himself, he naturally suspected treason in others. The man in due time returned, and reported that, although he had taken great pains to find out the truth, he was fully convinced, that not only were there no soldiers in the castle, but that it did not, to the best of his belief, contain an arm of any kind—the Innominato relying solely on his occult power for his defence.

Perfectly assured that he had no danger to apprehend, the baron left Lecco, attended by his retainers, and in a few hours afterwards he arrived at the Hospice, where his wish for an interview was conveyed to the astrologer. After some delay a reply was sent that the Innominato was willing to receive the baron on condition that he came alone, as his retainers would not be allowed to enter the castle. The baron hesitated for some moments, not liking to place himself in the power of a man who, after all, might prove a very dangerous adversary, and who might even use treacherous means. His love for Teresa Biffi, however, urged him to accept the invitation, and he accompanied the messenger to the castle.

The Innominato received his guest with stern courtesy; and, without even asking him to be seated, requested to know the object of his visit.

"Perhaps I am not altogether unknown to you," said the baron. "I am lord of the Engadin."

"Frankly," said the Innominato, "your name and reputation are both well known to me. It would give me great satisfaction were they less so."

"I regret to hear you speak in that tone," said the baron, evidently making great efforts to repress his rising passion. "A person in my position is not likely to be without enemies, but it rather surprises me to find a man of your reputation so prejudiced against me without having investigated the accusations laid to my charge."

"You judge wrongly if you imagine that I am so," said the

Innominato. "But once more, will you tell me the object of your visit?"

"I understood," said the baron, "by a message sent to me by the insolent inhabitants of Bormio, that you know the person with whom a young girl, named Teresa Biffi, is at present residing. Might I ask if that statement is correct?"

"I hardly sent it in those words," said the Innominato. "But admitting it to be so, I must first ask your reason for inquiring."

"I have not the slightest objection to inform you," said the baron. "I have nothing to conceal. I wish to make her my wife."

"On those terms I am willing to assist you," said the astrologer. "But only on the condition that you immediately release the messenger you have most unjustly confined in one of your dungeons, as well as the young son of the podesta, and that you grant them a safe escort back to Bormio; and further, that you promise to cease annoying the people of that district. Do all this, and I am willing to promise you that Teresa Biffi shall not only become your wife, but shall bring with her a dowry and wedding outfit sufficiently magnificent even for the exalted position to which you propose to raise her."

"I solemnly promise you," said the baron, "that the moment the wedding is over, the delegate from Bormio and the son of the podesta shall both leave my castle perfectly free and unhampered with any conditions; and moreover that I will send a strong escort with them to protect them on their road."

"I see you are already meditating treachery," said the Innominato. "But I will not, in any manner, alter my offer. The day week after their safe return to Bormio Teresa Biffi shall arrive at the castle of Gardonal for the wedding ceremony. Now you distinctly know my conditions, and I demand from you an unequivocal acceptance or refusal."

"What security shall I have that the bargain will be kept on your side?" said the baron.

"My word, and no other."

The baron remained silent for a moment, and then said—

"I accept your offer. But clearly understand me in my turn, sir astrologer. Fail to keep your promise, and had you ten times the power you have I will take my revenge on you; and I am not a man to threaten such a thing without doing it."

"All that I am ready to allow," said the Innominato, with great coolness; "that is to say, in case you have the power to carry out your threat, which in the present instance you have not. Do not imagine that because I am not surrounded by a band of armed cutthroats and miscreants I am not the stronger of the two. You little dream how powerless you are in my hands. You see this bird," he continued, taking down a common sparrow in a wooden cage from a nail in the wall on which it hung,— "it is not more helpless in my hands than you are; nay more, I will now give the bird far greater power over you than I possess over it."

As he spoke he unfastened the door of the cage, and the sparrow darted from it through the window into the air, and in a moment afterwards was lost to sight.

"That bird," the astrologer went on to say, "will follow you till I deprive it of the power. I bear you no malice for doubting my veracity. Falsehood is too much a portion of your nature for you to disbelieve its existence in others. I will not seek to punish you for the treachery which I am perfectly sure you will soon be imagining against me without giving you fair warning; for, a traitor yourself, you naturally suspect treason in others. As soon as you entertain a thought of evading your promise to release your prisoners, or conceive any treason or ill feeling against me, that sparrow will appear to you. If you instantly abandon the thought no harm will follow; but if you do not a terrible punishment will soon fall upon you. In whatever position you may find yourself at the moment, the bird will be near you, and no skill of yours will be able to harm it."

The baron now left the Innominato, and returned with his men to Lecco, where he employed himself for the remainder of the day in making preparations for his homeward journey. To return by the circuitous route he had taken in going to Lecco would have occupied too much time, as he was anxious to arrive at his castle, that he might without delay release the prisoners and make preparations for his wedding with Teresa Biffi. To pass the Valteline openly with his retainers—which was by far the shortest road—would have exposed him to too much danger; he therefore resolved to divide his party and send three men back by his brother's castle, so that they could return the horses they had borrowed. Then he would disguise himself and the fourth man (a German who could not speak a word of Italian, and from whom he had nothing therefore to fear on the score of treachery) as two Tyrolese merchants returning to their own country. He also purchased two mules and some provisions for the journey, so that they need not be obliged to rest in any of the villages they passed through, where possibly they might be detected, and probably maltreated.

Next morning the baron and his servant, together with the two mules, went on board a large bark which was manned by six men, and which he had hired for the occasion, and in it they started for Colico. At the commencement of their voyage they kept along the eastern side of the lake, but after advancing a few miles the wind, which had hitherto been moderate, now became so strong as to cause much fatigue to the rowers, and the captain of the bark determined on crossing the lake, so as to be under the lee of the mountains on the other side. When half way across they came in view of the turrets of the castle of the Innominato. The sight of the castle brought to the baron's mind his interview with its owner, and the defiant manner in which he had been treated by him. The longer he gazed the stronger became his anger against the Innominato, and at last it rose to such a point that he exclaimed aloud, to the great surprise of the men in the boat, "Some day I will meet thee again, thou insolent villain, and I will then take signal vengeance on thee for the insult offered me yesterday."

The words had hardly been uttered when a sparrow, apparently driven from the shore by the wind, settled on the bark for a moment, and then flew away. The baron instantly remembered what the Innominato had said to him, and also the warning the bird was to give. With a sensation closely resembling fear, he tried to change the current of his thoughts, and was on the point of turning his head from the castle, when the rowers in the boat simultaneously set up a loud shout of warning, and the baron then perceived that a heavily-laden vessel, four times the size of his own, and with a huge sail set, was running before the wind with great velocity, threatening the next moment to strike his boat on the beam; in which case both he and the men would undoubtedly be drowned. Fortunately, the captain of the strange bark had heard the cry of the rowers, and by rapidly putting down his helm saved their lives; though the baron's boat was struck with so much violence on the quarter that she nearly sank.

The Baron Conrad had now received an earnest that the threat of the Innominato was not a vain one, and feeling that he was entirely in his power, resolved if possible not to offend him again. The boat continued on her voyage, and late in the evening arrived safely at Colico, where the baron, with his servant and the mules, disembarked, and without delay proceeded on their journey. They continued on their road till nightfall, when they began to consider how they should pass the night. They looked around them, but they could perceive no habitation or shelter of any kind, and it was now raining heavily. They continued their journey onwards, and had almost come to the conclusion that they should be obliged to pass the night in the open air, when a short distance before them they saw a low cottage, the door of which was open, showing the dim light of a fire burning within. The baron now determined to ask the owner of the cottage for permission to remain there for the night; but to be certain that no danger could arise, he sent forward his man to discover whether it was a house standing by itself, or one of a village; as in the latter case he would have to use great caution to avoid being detected. His servant accordingly left him to obey orders, and shortly afterwards returned with the news that the house was a solitary one, and that he could not distinguish a trace of any other in the neighbourhood. Satisfied with this information, the baron proceeded to the cottage door, and begged the inmates to afford him shelter for the night, assuring them that the next morning he would remunerate them handsomely. The peasant and his wife—a sickly-looking, emaciated old couple—gladly offered them all the accommodation the wretched cabin could afford. After fastening up the mules at the back of the house, and bringing in the baggage and some dry fodder to form a bed for the baron and his servant, they prepared some of the food their guests had brought with them for supper, and shortly afterwards the baron and his servant were fast asleep.

Next morning they rose early and continued on their journey. After they had been some hours on the road, the baron, who had before been conversing with his retainer, suddenly became silent and absorbed in thought. He rode on a few paces in advance of the man, thinking over the conditions made by the Innominato, when the idea struck him whether it would not be possible in some way to evade them. He had hardly entertained the thought, when the sparrow flew rapidly before his mule's head, and then instantly afterwards his servant, who had ridden up to him, touched him on the shoulder and pointed to a body of eight or ten armed men about a quarter of a mile distant, who were advancing towards them. The baron, fearing lest they might be some of the armed inhabitants of the neighbourhood who were banded together against him, and seeing that no time was to be lost, immediately plunged, with his servant, into a thick copse where, without being seen, he could command a view of the advancing soldiers as they passed. He perceived that when they came near the place where he was concealed they halted, and evidently set about examining the traces of the footsteps of the mules. They communed together for some time as if in doubt what course they should adopt, and finally, the leader giving the order, they continued their march onwards, and the baron shortly afterwards left his place of concealment.

Nothing further worthy of notice occurred that day; and late at night they passed through Bormio, fortunately without being observed. They afterwards arrived safely at the foot of the mountain pass, and at dawn began the ascent. The day was fine and calm, and the sun shone magnificently The baron, who now calculated that the dangers of his journey were over, was in high spirits, and familiarly conversed with his retainer. When they had reached a considerable elevation, the path narrowed, so that the two could not ride abreast, and the baron went in advance. He now became very silent and thoughtful, all his thoughts being fixed on the approaching wedding, and in speculations as to how short a time it would take for the delegate and the youth to reach Bormio. Suddenly the thought occurred to him, whether the men whom he should send to escort the hostages back, could not, when they had completed their business, remain concealed in the immediate neighbourhood till after the celebration of the wedding, and then bring back with them some other hostage, and thus enable him to make further demands for compensation for the insult he considered had been offered him. Although the idea had only been vaguely formed, and possibly with but little intention of carrying it out, he had an immediate proof that the power of the astrologer was following him. A sparrow settled on the ground before him, and did not move until his mule was close to it, when it rose in the air right before his face. He continued to follow its course with his eyes, and as it rose higher he thought he perceived a tremulous movement in an immense mass of snow, which had accumulated at the base of one of the mountain peaks. All thought of treachery immediately vanished. He gave a cry of alarm to his servant, and they both hurried onwards, thus barely escaping being buried in an avalanche, which the moment afterwards overwhelmed the path they had crossed.

The baron was now more convinced than ever of the tremendous power of the Innominato, and so great was his fear of him, that he resolved for the future not to contemplate any treachery against him, or entertain any thoughts of revenge.

The day after the baron's arrival at the castle of Gardonal, he ordered the delegate and the podesta's son to be brought into his presence. Assuming a tone of much mildness and courtesy, he told them he much regretted the inconvenience they had been put to, but that the behaviour of the inhabitants of Bormio had left him no alternative. He was ready to admit that the delegate had told him the truth, although from the interview he had with the Innominato, he was by no means certain that the inhabitants of their town had acted in a friendly manner towards him, or were without blame in the matter. Still he did not wish to be harsh, and was willing for the future to be on friendly terms with them if they promised to cease insulting him—what possible affront they could have offered him it would be difficult to say. "At the same time, in justice to myself," he continued (his natural cupidity gaining the ascendant at the moment), "I hardly think I ought to allow you to return without the payment of some fair ransom."

He had scarcely uttered these words when a sparrow flew in at the window, and darting wildly two or three times across the hall, left by the same window through which it had entered. Those present who noticed the bird looked at it with an eye of indifference—but not so the baron. He knew perfectly well that it was a warning from the astrologer, and he looked around him to see what accident might have befallen him had he continued the train of thought. Nothing of an extraordinary nature followed the disappearance of the bird. The baron now changed the conversation, and told his prisoners that they were at liberty to depart as soon as they pleased; and that to prevent any misfortune befalling them on the road, he would send four of his retainers to protect them. In this he kept his promise to the letter, and a few days afterwards the men returned, reporting that the delegate and the son of the podesta had both arrived safely at their destination.

Part III

Immediately after the departure of his prisoners, the baron began to make preparations for his wedding, for although he detested the Innominato in his heart, he had still the fullest reliance on his fulfilling the promise he had made. His assurance was further confirmed by a messenger from the astrologer to inform him that on the next Wednesday the affianced bride would arrive with her suite, and that he (the Innominato) had given this notice, that all things might be in readiness for the ceremony.

Neither expense nor exertion was spared by the baron to make his nuptials imposing and magnificent. The chapel belonging to the castle, which had been allowed to fall into a most neglected condition, was put into order, the altar redecorated, and the walls hung with tapestry. Preparations were made in the inner hall for a banquet on the grandest scale, which was to be given after the ceremony; and on a dais in the main hall into which the bride was to be conducted on her arrival were placed two chairs of state, where the baron and his bride were to be seated.

When the day arrived for the wedding, everything was prepared for the reception of the bride. As no hour had been named for her arrival, all persons who were to be engaged in the ceremony were ready in the castle by break of day; and the baron, in a state of great excitement, mounted to the top of the watch-tower, that he might be able to give orders to the rest the moment her cavalcade appeared in sight. Hour after hour passed, but still Teresa did not make her appearance, and at last the baron began to feel considerable anxiety on the subject.

At last a mist, which had been over a part of the valley, cleared up, and all the anxiety of the baron was dispelled; for in the distance he perceived a group of travellers approaching the castle, some mounted on horseback and some on foot. In front rode the bride on a superb white palfrey, her face covered with a thick veil. On each side of her rode an esquire magnificently dressed. Behind her were a waiting woman on horseback and two men-servants; and in the rear were several led mules laden with packages. The baron now quitted his position in the tower and descended to the castle gates to receive his bride. When he arrived there, he found one of the esquires, who had ridden forward at the desire of his mistress, waiting to speak to him.

"I have been ordered," he said to the baron, "by the Lady Teresa, to request that you will be good enough to allow her to change her dress before she meets you."

The baron of course willingly assented, and then retired into the hall destined for the reception ceremony. Shortly afterwards Teresa arrived at the castle, and being helped from her palfrey, she proceeded with her lady in waiting and a female attendant (who had been engaged by the baron) into her private apartment, while two of the muleteers brought up a large trunk containing her wedding dress.

In less than an hour Teresa left her room to be introduced to the baron, and was conducted into his presence by one of the esquires. As soon as she entered the hall, a cry of admiration arose from all present—so extraordinary was her beauty. The baron, in a state of breathless emotion, advanced to meet her, but before he had reached her she bent on her knee, and remained in that position till he had raised her up. "Kneel not to me, thou lovely one," he said. "It is for all present to kneel to thee in adoration of thy wonderful beauty, rather than for thee to bend to any one." So saying, and holding her hand, he led her to one of the seats on the daïs, and then, seating himself by her side, gave orders for the ceremony of introduction to begin. One by one the different persons to be presented were led up to her, all of whom she received with a grace and amiability which raised her very high in their estimation.

When the ceremony of introduction was over the baron ordered that the procession should be formed, and then, taking Teresa by the hand, he led her into the chapel, followed by the others. When all were arranged in their proper places the marriage ceremony was performed by the priest, and the newly-married couple, with the retainers and guests, entered into the banqueting hall. Splendid as was the repast which had been prepared for the company, their attention seemed for some time more drawn to the baron and his bride than to the duties of the feast. A handsomer couple it would have been impossible to find. The baron himself, as has been stated already, had no lack of manly beauty either in face or form; while the loveliness of his bride appeared almost more than mortal. Even their splendid attire seemed to attract little notice when compared with their personal beauty.

After the surprise and admiration had somewhat abated, the feast progressed most satisfactorily. All were in high spirits, and good humour and conviviality reigned throughout the hall. Even on the baron it seemed to produce a kindly effect, so that few who could have seen him at that moment would have imagined him to be the stern, cold-blooded tyrant he really was. His countenance was lighted up with good humour and friendliness. Much as his attention was occupied with his bride, he had still a little to bestow on his guests, and he rose many times from his seat to request the attention of the servants to their wants. At last he cast his eye over the tables as if searching for some person whom he could not see, and he then beckoned to the major domo, who, staff of office in hand, advanced to receive his orders.

"I do not see the esquires of the Lady Teresa in the room," said the baron.

"Your excellency," said the man, "they are not here."

"How is that?" said the baron, with some impatience. "You ought to have found room for them in the hall. Where are they?"

"Your excellency," said the major domo, who from the expression of the baron's countenance evidently expected a storm, "they are not here. The whole of the suite left the castle immediately after the mules were unladen and her ladyship had left her room. I was inspecting the places which I had prepared for them, when a servant came forward and told me that the esquires and attendants had left the castle. I at once hurried after them and begged they would return, as I was sure your excellency would feel hurt if they did not stay to the banquet. But they told me they had received express orders to leave the castle directly after they had seen the Lady Teresa lodged safely in it. I again entreated them to stay, but it was useless. They hurried on their way, and I returned by myself."

"The ill-bred hounds!" said the baron, in anger. "A sound scourging would have taught them better manners."

"Do not be angry with them," said Teresa, laying her hand gently on that of her husband's; "they did but obey their master's orders."

"Some day, I swear," said the baron, "I will be revenged on their master for this insult, miserable churl that he is!"

He had no sooner uttered these words than he looked round him for the sparrow, but the bird did not make its appearance. Possibly its absence alarmed him even more than its presence would have done, for he began to dread lest the vengeance of the astrologer was about to fall on him, without giving him the usual notice. Teresa, perceiving the expression of his countenance, did all in her power to calm him, but for some time she but partially succeeded. He continued to glance anxiously about him, to ascertain, if possible, from which side the blow might come. He was just on the point of raising a goblet to his lips, when the idea seized him that the wine might be poisoned. He declined to touch food for the same reason. The idea of being struck with death when at the height of his happiness seemed to overwhelm him. Thanks, however, to the kind soothing of Teresa, as well as the absence of any visible effects of the Innominato's anger, he at last became completely reassured, and the feast proceeded.

Long before the banquet had concluded the baron and his wife quitted the hall and retired through their private apartments to the terrace of the castle. The evening, which was now rapidly advancing, was warm and genial, and not a cloud was to be seen in the atmosphere. For some time they walked together up and down on the terrace; and afterwards they seated themselves on a bench. There, with his arm round her waist and her head leaning on his shoulder, they watched the sun in all his magnificence sinking behind the mountains. The sun had almost disappeared, when the baron took his wife's hand in his.

"How cold thou art, my dear!" he said to her. "Let us go in."

Teresa made no answer, but rising from her seat was conducted by her husband into the room which opened on to the terrace, and which was lighted by a large brass lamp which hung by a chain from the ceiling. When they were nearly under the lamp, whose light increased as the daylight declined, Conrad again cast his arm round his wife, and fondly pressed her head to his breast. They remained thus for some moments, entranced in their happiness.

"Dost thou really love me, Teresa!" asked the baron.

"Love you?" said Teresa, now burying her face in his bosom. "Love you? Yes, dearer than all the world. My very existence hangs on your life. When that ceases my existence ends."

When she had uttered these words, Conrad, in a state of intense happiness, said to her—

"Kiss me, my beloved."

Teresa still kept her face pressed on his bosom; and Conrad, to overcome her coyness, placed his hand on her head and gently pressed it backwards, so that he might kiss her.

He stood motionless, aghast with horror, for the light of the lamp above their heads showed him no longer the angelic features of Teresa but the hideous face of a corpse that had remained some time in the tomb, and whose only sign of vitality was a horrible phosphoric light which shone in its eyes. Conrad now tried to rush from the room, and to scream for assistance—but in vain. With one arm she clasped him tightly round the waist, and raising the other, she placed her clammy hand upon his mouth, and threw him with great force upon the floor. Then seizing the side of his neck with her lips, she deliberately and slowly sucked from him his life's blood; while he, utterly incapable either of moving or crying, was yet perfectly conscious of the awful fate that was awaiting him.

In this manner Conrad remained for some hours in the arms of his vampire wife. At last faintness came over him, and he grew insensible. The sun had risen some hours before consciousness returned. He rose from the ground horror-stricken and pallid, and glanced fearfully around him to see if Teresa were still there; but he found himself alone in the room. For some minutes he remained undecided what step to take. At last he rose from his chair to leave the apartment, but he was so weak he could scarcely drag himself along. When he left the room he bent his steps towards the court-yard. Each person he met saluted him with the most profound respect, while on the countenance of each was visible an expression of intense surprise, so altered was he from the athletic young man they had seen him the day before. Presently he heard the merry laughter of a number of children, and immediately hastened to the spot from whence the noise came. To his surprise he found his wife Teresa, in full possession of her beauty, playing with several children, whose mothers had brought them to see her, and who stood delighted with the condescending kindness of the baroness towards their little ones.

Conrad remained motionless for some moments, gazing with intense surprise at his wife, and the idea occurred to him that the events of the last night must have been a terrible dream and nothing more. But he was at a loss how to account for his bodily weakness? Teresa, in the midst of her gambols with the children, accidentally raised her head and perceived her husband. She uttered a slight cry of pleasure when she saw him, and snatching up in her arms a beautiful child she had been playing with, she rushed towards him, exclaiming—

"Look, dear Conrad, what a little beauty this is! Is he not a little cherub?"

The baron gazed wildly at his wife for a few moments, but said nothing.

"My dearest husband, what ails you?" said Teresa. "Are you not well?"

Conrad made no answer, but turning suddenly round staggered hurriedly away, while Teresa, with an expression of alarm and anxiety on her face, followed him with her eyes as he went. He still hurried on till he reached the small sitting-room from which he was accustomed each morning to issue his orders to his dependants, and seated himself in a chair to recover if possible from the bewilderment he was in. Presently Ludovico, whose duty it was to attend on his master every morning for instructions, entered the room, and bowing respectfully to the baron, stood silently aside, waiting till he should be spoken to, but during the time marking the baron's altered appearance with the most intense curiosity. After some moments the baron asked him what he saw to make him stare in that manner.

"Pardon my boldness, your excellency," said Ludovico, "but I was afraid you might be ill. I trust I am in error."

"What should make you think I am unwell?" inquired the baron.

"Your highness's countenance is far paler than usual, and there is a small wound on the side of your throat. I hope you have not injured yourself."

The last remark of Ludovico decided the baron that the events of the evening had been no hallucination. What stronger proof could be required than the marks of his vampire wife's teeth still upon him? He perceived that some course of action must be at once decided upon, and the urgency of his position aided him to concentrate his thoughts. He determined on visiting a celebrated anchorite who lived in the mountains about four leagues distant, and who was famous not only for the piety of his life, but for his power in exorcising evil spirits. Having come to this resolution, he desired Ludovico immediately to saddle for him a sure-footed mule, as the path to the anchorite's dwelling was not only difficult but dangerous.

Ludovico bowed, and after having been informed that there were no other orders, he left the room, wondering in his mind what could be the reason for his master's wishing a mule saddled, when he generally rode only the highest-spirited horses. The conclusion he came to was, that the baron must have been attacked with some serious illness, and was about to proceed to some skilful leech.

As soon as Ludovico had left the room, the baron called to one of the servants whom he saw passing, and ordered breakfast to be brought to him immediately, hoping that by a hearty meal he should recover sufficient strength for the journey he was about to undertake. To a certain extent he succeeded, though possibly it was from the quantity of wine he drank, rather than from any other cause, for he had no appetite and had eaten but little.

He now descended into the courtyard of the castle, cautiously avoiding his wife. Finding the mule in readiness, he mounted it and started on his journey. For some time he went along quietly and slowly, for he still felt weak and languid, but as he attained a higher elevation of the mountains, the cold breeze seemed to invigorate him. He now began to consider how he could rid himself of the horrible vampire he had married, and of whose real nature he had no longer any doubt. Speculations on this subject occupied him till he had entered on a narrow path on the slope of an exceedingly high mountain. It was difficult to keep footing, and it required all his caution to prevent himself from falling. Of fear, however, the baron had none, and his thoughts continued to run on the possibility of separating himself from Teresa, and on what vengeance he would take on the Innominato for the treachery he had practised on him, as soon as he should be fairly freed. The more he dwelt on his revenge, the more excited he became, till a last he exclaimed aloud, "Infamous wretch! Let me be but once fairly released from the execrable fiend you have imposed upon me, and I swear I will burn thee alive in thy castle, as a fitting punishment for the sorcery thou hast practised."

Conrad had hardly uttered these words, when the pathway upon which he was riding gave way beneath him, and glided down the incline into a tremendous precipice below. He succeeded in throwing himself from his mule, which, with the débris of the rocks, was hurried over the precipice, while he clutched with the energy of despair at each object he saw likely to give him a moment's support. But everything he touched gave way, and he gradually sank and sank towards the verge of the precipice, his efforts to save himself becoming more violent the nearer he approached to what appeared certain death. Down he sank, till his legs actually hung over the precipice, when he succeeded in grasping a stone somewhat firmer than the others, thus retarding his fall for a moment. In horror he now glanced at the terrible chasm beneath him, when suddenly different objects came before his mind with fearful reality. There was an unhappy peasant, who had without permission killed a head of game, hanging from the branch of a tree still struggling in the agonies of death, while his wife and children were in vain imploring the baron's clemency.

This vanished and he saw a boy with a knife in his hand, stabbing at his own mother for some slight offence she had given him.

This passed, and he found himself in a small village, the inhabitants of which were all dead within their houses; for at the approach of winter he had, in a fit of ill-temper, ordered his retainers to take from them all their provisions; and a snowstorm coming on immediately afterwards, they were blocked up in their dwellings, and all perished.

Again his thoughts reverted to the position he was in, and his eye glanced over the terrible precipice that yawned beneath him, when he saw, as if in a dream, the house of Biffi the farmer, with his wife and children around him, apparently contented and happy.

As soon as he had realized the idea, the stone which he had clutched began to give way, and all seemed lost to him, when a sparrow suddenly flew on the earth a short distance from him, and immediately afterwards darted away "Save but my life!" screamed the baron, "and I swear I will keep all secret."

The words had hardly been uttered, when a goatherd with a long staff in his hand appeared on the incline above him. The man perceiving the imminent peril of the baron, with great caution, and yet with great activity, descended to assist him. He succeeded in reaching a ledge of rock a few feet above, and rather to the side of the baron, to whom he stretched forth the long mountain staff in his hand. The baron clutched it with such energy as would certainly have drawn the goatherd over with him, had it not been that the latter was a remarkably powerful man. With some difficulty the baron reached the ledge of the rock, and the goatherd then ascended to a higher position, and in like manner drew the baron on, till at last he had contrived to get him to a place of safety. As soon as Conrad found himself out of danger, he gazed wildly around him for a moment, then dizziness came over him, and he sank fainting on the ground.

When the baron had recovered his senses, he found himself so weak that it would have been impossible for him to have reached the castle that evening. He therefore willingly accompanied the goatherd to his hut in the mountains, where he proposed to pass the night. The man made what provision he could for his illustrious guest, and prepared him a supper of the best his hut afforded; but had the latter been composed of the most exquisite delicacies, it would have been equally tasteless; for Conrad had not the slightest appetite. Evening was now rapidly approaching, and the goatherd prepared a bed of leaves, over which he threw a cloak, and the baron, utterly exhausted, reposed on it for the night, without anything occurring to disturb his rest.

Next morning he found himself somewhat refreshed by his night's rest, and he prepared to return to the castle, assisted by the goatherd, to whom he had promised a handsome reward. He had now given up all idea of visiting the anchorite, dreading that by so doing he might excite the animosity of the Innominato, of whose tremendous power he had lately received more than ample proof. In due time he reached home in safety, and the goatherd was dismissed after having received the promised reward. On entering the castle-yard the baron found his wife in a state of great alarm and sorrow, and surrounded by the retainers. No sooner did she perceive her husband, than, uttering a cry of delight and surprise, she rushed forward to clasp him in her arms; but the baron pushed her rudely away, and hurrying forwards, directed his steps to the room in which he was accustomed to issue his orders. Ludovico, having heard of the arrival of his master, immediately waited on him.

"Ludovico," said the baron, as soon as he saw him, "I want you to execute an order for me with great promptitude and secrecy. Go below, and prepare two good horses for a journey; one for you, the other for myself. See that we take with us provisions and equipments for two or three days. As soon as they are in readiness, leave the castle with them without speaking to any one, and wait for me about a league up the mountain, where in less than two hours I will join you. Now see that you faithfully carry out my orders, and if you do so, I assure you you will lose nothing by your obedience."

Ludovico left the baron's presence to execute his order, when immediately afterwards a servant came into the room, and inquired if the Lady Teresa might enter.

"Tell your mistress," said the baron, in a tone of great courtesy and kindness, "that I hope she will excuse me for the moment, as I am deeply engaged in affairs of importance; but I shall await her visit with great impatience in the afternoon."

The baron now left to himself, began to draw out more fully the plan for his future operations. He resolved to visit his brother Hermann, and consult him as to what steps he ought to take in this horrible emergency; and in case no better means presented themselves, he determined on offering to give up to Hermann the castle of Gardonal and the whole valley of the Engadin, on condition of receiving from him an annuity sufficient to support him in the position he had always been accustomed to maintain. He then intended to retire to some distant country, where there would be no probability of his being followed by the horrible monster whom he had accepted as his wife. Of course he had no intention of receiving Teresa in the afternoon, and he had merely put off her visit the purpose of allowing himself to escape with greater convenience from the castle.

About an hour after Ludovico had left him, the baron quitted the castle by a postern, with as much haste as his enfeebled strength would allow, and hurried after his retainer, whom he found awaiting him with the horses. The baron immediately mounted one, and followed by Ludovico, took the road to his brother's, where in three days he arrived in safety. Hermann received his brother with great pleasure, though much surprised at the alteration in his appearance.

"My dear Conrad," he said to him, "what can possibly have occurred to you? You look very pale, weak, and haggard. Have you been ill?"

"Worse, a thousand times worse," said Conrad. "Let us go where we may be by ourselves, and I will tell you all."

Hermann led his brother into a private room, where Conrad explained to him the terrible misfortune which had befallen him. Hermann listened attentively, and for some time could not help doubting whether his brother's mind was not affected; but Conrad explained everything in so circumstantial and lucid a manner as to dispel that idea. To the proposition which Conrad made, to make over the territory of the Engadin Valley for an annuity, Hermann promised to give full consideration. At the same time, before any further steps were taken in the matter, he advised Conrad to visit a villa he had, on the sea-shore, about ten miles distant from Genoa; where, in quiet and seclusion, he would be able to recover his energies.

Conrad thanked his brother for his advice, and willingly accepted the offer. Two days afterwards he started on the journey, and by the end of the week arrived safely, and without difficulty, at the villa.

On the evening of his arrival, Conrad, who had employed himself during the afternoon in visiting the different apartments as well as the grounds surrounding the villa, was seated at a window overlooking the sea. The evening was deliciously calm, and he felt such ease and security as he had not enjoyed for some time past. The sun was sinking in the ocean, and the moon began to appear, and the stars one by one to shine in the cloudless heavens. The thought crossed Conrad's mind that the sight of the sun sinking in the waters strongly resembled his own position when he fell over the precipice. The thought had hardly been conceived when some one touched him on the shoulder. He turned round, and saw standing before him, in the full majesty of her beauty—his wife Teresa!

"My dearest Conrad," she said, with much affection in her tone, "why have you treated me in this cruel manner? It was most unkind of you to leave me suddenly without giving the slightest hint of your intentions."

"Execrable fiend," said Conrad, springing from his chair, "leave me! Why do you haunt me in this manner?"

"Do not speak so harshly to me, my dear husband," said Teresa. "To oblige you I was taken from my grave; and on you now my very existence depends."

"Rather my death," said Conrad. "One night more such as we passed, and I should be a corpse."

"Nay, dear Conrad," said Teresa; "I have the power of indefinitely prolonging your life. Drink but of this," she continued, taking from the table behind her a silver goblet, "and tomorrow all ill effects will have passed away."

Conrad mechanically took the goblet from her hand, and was on the point of raising it to his lips when he suddenly stopped, and with a shudder replaced it again on the table.

"It is blood," he said.

"True, my dear husband," said Teresa; "what else could it be? My life is dependent on your life's blood, and when that ceases so does my life. Drink then, I implore you," she continued, again offering him the goblet. "Look, the sun has already sunk beneath the wave; a minute more and daylight will have gone. Drink, Conrad, I implore you, or this night will be your last."

Conrad again took the goblet from her hand to raise it to his lips; but it was impossible, and he placed it on the table. A ray of pure moonlight now penetrated the room, as if to prove that the light of day had fled. Teresa, again transformed into a horrible vampire, flew at her husband, and throwing him on the floor, fastened her teeth on the half-healed wound in his throat. The next morning, when the servants entered the room, they found the baron a corpse on the floor; but Teresa was nowhere to be seen, nor was she ever heard of afterwards.

Little more remains to be told. Hermann took possession of the castle of Gardonal and the Valley of the Engadin, and treated his vassals with even more despotism than his brother had done before him. At last, driven to desperation, they rose against him and slew him; and the valley afterwards became absorbed into the Canton of the Grisons.

Let Loose

by Mary Cholmondeley

The dead abide with us! Though stark and cold
Earth seems to grip them, they are with us still.

Some years ago I took up architecture, and made a tour through Holland, studying the buildings of that interesting country. I was not then aware that it is not enough to take up art. Art must take you up, too. I never doubted but that my passing enthusiasm for her would be returned. When I discovered that she was a stern mistress, who did not immediately respond to my attentions, I naturally transferred them to another shrine. There are other things in the world besides art. I am now a landscape gardener.

But at the time of which I write I was engaged in a violent flirtation with architecture. I had one companion on this expedition, who has since become one of the leading architects of the day. He was a thin, determined-looking man with a screwed-up face and heavy jaw, slow of speech, and absorbed in his work to a degree which I quickly found tiresome. He was possessed of a certain quiet power of overcoming obstacles which I have rarely seen equalled. He has since become my brother-in-law, so I ought to know; for my parents did not like him much and opposed the marriage, and my sister did not like him at all, and refused him over and over again; but, nevertheless, he eventually married her.

I have thought since that one of his reasons for choosing me as his travelling companion on this occasion was because he was getting up steam for what he subsequently termed "an alliance with my family," but the idea never entered my head at the time. A more careless man as to dress I have rarely met, and yet, in all the heat of July in Holland, I noticed that he never appeared without a high, starched collar, which had not even fashion to commend it at that time.

I often chaffed him about his splendid collars, and asked him why he wore them, but without eliciting any response. One evening, as we were walking back to our lodgings in Middeburg, I attacked him for about the thirtieth time on the subject.

"Why on earth do you wear them?" I said. "You have, I believe, asked me that question many times," he replied, in his slow, precise utterance; "but always on occasions when I was occupied. I am now at leisure, and I will tell you."

And he did.

I have put down what he said, as nearly in his own words as I can remember them.

Ten years ago, I was asked to read a paper on English Frescoes at the Institute of British Architects. I was determined to make the paper as good as I could, down to the slightest details, and I consulted many books on the subject, and studied every fresco I could find. My father, who had been an architect, had left me, at his death, all his papers and note-books on the subject of architecture. I searched them diligently, and found in one of them a slight unfinished sketch of nearly fifty years ago that specially interested me. Underneath was noted, in his clear, small hand— Frescoed east wall of crypt. Parish Church. Wet Waste-on-the-Wolds, Yorkshire (viâ Pickering).

The sketch had such a fascination for me that I decided to go there and see the fresco for myself. I had only a very vague idea as to where Wet Waste-on-the-Wolds was, but I was ambitious for the success of my paper; it was hot in London, and I set off on my long journey not without a certain degree of pleasure, with my dog

Brian, a large nondescript brindled creature, as my only companion.

I reached Pickering, in Yorkshire, in the course of the after-noon, and then began a series of experiments on local lines which ended, after several hours, in my finding myself deposited at a little out-of-the-world station within nine or ten miles of Wet Waste. As no conveyance of any kind was to be had, I shouldered my port-manteau, and set out on a long white road that stretched away into the distance over the bare, treeless wold. I must have walked for several hours, over a waste of moorland patched with heather, when a doctor passed me, and gave me a lift to within a mile of my destination. The mile was a long one, and it was quite dark by the time I saw the feeble glimmer of lights in front of me, and found that I had reached Wet Waste. I had considerable difficulty in get-ting any one to take me in; but at last I persuaded the owner of the public-house to give me a bed, and, quite tired out, I got into it as soon as possible, for fear he should change his mind, and fell asleep to the sound of a little stream below my window.

I was up early next morning, and inquired directly after break-fast the way to the clergyman's house, which I found was close at hand. At Wet Waste everything was close at hand. The whole vil-lage seemed composed of a straggling row of one-storeyed grey stone houses, the same colour as the stone walls that separated the few fields enclosed from the surrounding waste, and as the little bridges over the beck that ran down one side of the grey wide street. Everything was grey. The church, the low tower of which I could see at a little distance, seemed to have been built of the same stone; so was the parsonage when I came up to it, accompanied on my way by a mob of rough, uncouth children, who eyed me and Brian with half-defiant curiosity.

The clergyman was at home, and after a short delay I was admitted. Leaving Brian in charge of my drawing materials, I fol-lowed the servant into a low panelled room, in which, at a latticed window, a very old man was sitting. The morning light fell on his white head bent low over a litter of papers and books.

"Mr. er—?" he said, looking up slowly, with one finger keeping his place in a book.

"Blake."

"Blake," he repeated after me, and was silent.

I told him that I was an architect; that I had come to study a fresco in the crypt of his church, and asked for the keys.

"The crypt," he said, pushing up his spectacles and peering hard at me. "The crypt has been closed for thirty years. Ever since—" and he stopped short.

"I should be much obliged for the keys," I said again. He shook his head.

"No," he said. "No one goes in there now."

"It is a pity," I remarked, "for I have come a long way with that one object"; and I told him about the paper I had been asked to read, and the trouble I was taking with it.

He became interested. "Ah!" he said, laying down his pen, and removing his finger from the page before him, "I can understand that. I also was young once, and fired with ambition. The lines have fallen to me in somewhat lonely places, and for forty years I have held the cure of souls in this place, where, truly, I have seen but little of the world, though I myself may be not unknown in the paths of literature. Possibly you may have read a pamphlet, written by myself, on the Syrian version of the Three Authentic Epistles of Ignatius?"

"Sir," I said, "I am ashamed to confess that I have not time to read even the most celebrated books. My one object in life is my art. Ars longa, vita brevis, you know."

"You are right, my son," said the old man, evidently disappointed, but looking at me kindly. "There are diversities of gifts, and if the Lord has entrusted you with a talent, look to it. Lay it not up in a napkin."

I said I would not do so if he would lend me the keys of the crypt. He seemed startled by my recurrence to the subject and looked undecided.

"Why not?" he murmured to himself. "The youth appears a good youth. And superstition! What is it but distrust in God!"

He got up slowly, and taking a large bunch of keys out of his pocket, opened with one of them an oak cupboard in the corner of the room.

"They should be here," he muttered, peering in; "but the dust of many years deceives the eye. See, my son, if among these parchments there be two keys; one of iron and very large, and the other steel, and of a long thin appearance."

I went eagerly to help him, and presently found in a back drawer two keys tied together, which he recognised at once.

"Those are they," he said. "The long one opens the first door at the bottom of the steps which go down against the outside wall of the church hard by the sword graven in the wall. The second opens (but it is hard of opening and of shutting) the iron door within the passage leading to the crypt itself. My son, is it necessary to your treatise that you should enter this crypt?"

I replied that it was absolutely necessary.

"Then take them," he said, "and in the evening you will bring them to me again."

I said I might want to go several days running, and asked if he would not allow me to keep them till I had finished my work; but on that point he was firm.

"Likewise," he added, "be careful that you lock the first door at the foot of the steps before you unlock the second, and lock the second also while you are within. Furthermore, when you come out lock the iron inner door as well as the wooden one."

I promised I would do so, and, after thanking him, hurried away, delighted at my success in obtaining the keys. Finding Brian and my sketching materials waiting for me in the porch, I eluded the vigilance of my escort of children by taking the narrow private path between the parsonage and the church which was close at hand, standing in a quadrangle of ancient yews.

The church itself was interesting, and I noticed that it must have arisen out of the ruins of a previous building, judging from the number of fragments of stone caps and arches, bearing traces of very early carving, now built into the walls. There were incised crosses, too, in some places, and one especially caught my attention, being flanked by a large sword. It was in trying to get a nearer look at this that I stumbled, and, looking down, saw at my feet a flight of narrow stone steps green with moss and mildew. Evidently this was the entrance to the crypt. I at once descended the steps, taking care of my footing, for they were damp and slippery in the extreme. Brian accompanied me, as nothing would induce him to remain behind. By the time I had reached the bottom of the stairs, I found myself almost in darkness, and I had to strike a light before I could find the keyhole and the proper key to fit into it. The door, which was of wood, opened inwards fairly easily, although an accumulation of mould and rubbish on the ground outside showed it had not been used for many years. Having got through it, which was not altogether an easy matter, as nothing would induce it to open more than about eighteen inches, I carefully locked it behind me, although I should have preferred to leave it open, as there is to some minds an unpleasant feeling in being locked in anywhere, in case of a sudden exit seeming advisable.

I kept my candle alight with some difficulty, and after groping my way down a low and of course exceedingly dank passage, came to another door. A toad was squatting against it, who looked as if he had been sitting there about a hundred years. As I lowered the candle to the floor, he gazed at the light with unblinking eyes, and then retreated slowly into a crevice in the wall, leaving against the door a small cavity in the dry mud which had gradually silted up round his person. I noticed that this door was of iron, and had a long bolt, which, however, was broken. Without delay, I fitted the second key into the lock, and pushing the door open after considerable difficulty, I felt the cold breath of the crypt upon my face. I must own I experienced a momentary regret at locking the second door again as soon as I was well inside, but I felt it my duty to do so. Then, leaving the key in the lock, I seized my candle and looked round. I was standing in a low vaulted chamber with groined roof, cut out of the solid rock. It was difficult to see where the crypt ended, as further light thrown on any point only showed other rough archways or openings, cut in the rock, which had probably served at one time for family vaults. A peculiarity of the Wet Waste crypt, which I had not noticed in other places of that description, was the tasteful arrangement of skulls and bones which were packed about four feet high on either side. The skulls were symmetrically built up to within a few inches of the top of the low archway on my left, and the shin bones were arranged in the same manner on my right. But the fresco! I looked round for it in vain. Perceiving at the further end of the crypt a very low and very massive archway, the entrance to which was not filled up with bones, I passed under it, and found myself in a second smaller chamber. Holding my candle above my head, the first object its light fell upon was—the fresco, and at a glance I saw that it was unique. Setting down some of my things with a trembling hand on a rough stone shelf hard by, which had evidently been a credence table, I examined the work more closely. It was a reredos over what had probably been the altar at the time the priests were proscribed. The fresco belonged to the earliest part of the fifteenth century, and was so perfectly preserved that I could almost trace the limits of each day's work in the plaster, as the artist had dashed it on and smoothed it out with his trowel. The subject was the Ascension, gloriously treated. I can hardly describe my elation as I stood and looked at it, and reflected that this magnificent specimen of English fresco painting would be made known to the world by myself. Recollecting myself at last, I opened my sketching bag, and, lighting all the candles I had brought with me, set to work.

Brian walked about near me, and though I was not otherwise than glad of his company in my rather lonely position, I wished several times I had left him behind. He seemed restless, and even the sight of so many bones appeared to exercise no soothing effect upon him. At last, however, after repeated commands, he lay down, watchful but motionless, on the stone floor.

I must have worked for several hours, and I was pausing to rest my eyes and hands, when I noticed for the first time the intense stillness that surrounded me. No sound from me reached the outer world. The church clock which had clanged out so loud and ponderously as I went down the steps, had not since sent the faintest whisper of its iron tongue down to me below. All was silent as the grave. This was the grave. Those who had come here had indeed gone down into silence. I repeated the words to myself, or rather they repeated themselves to me.

Gone down into silence.

I was awakened from my reverie by a faint sound. I sat still and listened. Bats occasionally frequent vaults and underground places.

The sound continued, a faint, stealthy, rather unpleasant sound. I do not know what kinds of sounds bats make, whether pleasant or otherwise. Suddenly there was a noise as of something falling, a momentary pause and then—an almost imperceptible but distant jangle as of a key.

I had left the key in the lock after I had turned it, and I now regretted having done so. I got up, took one of the candles, and went back into the larger crypt—for though I trust I am not so effeminate as to be rendered nervous by hearing a noise for which I cannot instantly account; still, on occasions of this kind, I must honestly say I should prefer that they did not occur. As I came towards the iron door, there was another distinct (I had almost said hurried) sound. The impression on my mind was one of great haste. When I reached the door, and held the candle near the lock to take out the key, I perceived that the other one, which hung by a short string to its fellow, was vibrating slightly. I should have preferred not to find it vibrating, as there seemed no occasion for such a course; but I put them both into my pocket, and turned to go back to my work. As I turned, I saw on the ground what had occasioned the louder noise I had heard, namely, a skull which had evidently just slipped from its place on the top of one of the walls of bones, and had rolled almost to my feet. There, disclosing a few more inches of the top of an archway behind, was the place from which it had been dislodged. I stooped to pick it up, but fearing to displace any more skulls by meddling with the pile, and not liking to gather up its scattered teeth, I let it lie, and went back to my work, in which I was soon so completely absorbed that I was only roused at last by my candles beginning to burn low and go out one after another.

Then, with a sigh of regret, for I had not nearly finished, I turned to go. Poor Brian, who had never quite reconciled himself to the place, was beside himself with delight. As I opened the iron door he pushed past me, and a moment later I heard him whining and scratching, and I had almost added, beating, against the wooden one. I locked the iron door, and hurried down the passage as quickly as I could, and almost before I had got the other one ajar there seemed to be a rush past me into the open air, and Brian was bounding up the steps and out of sight. As I stopped to take out the key, I felt quite deserted and left behind. When I came out once more into the sunlight, there was a vague sensation all about me in the air of exultant freedom.

It was already late in the afternoon, and after I had sauntered back to the parsonage to give up the keys, I persuaded the people of the public-house to let me join in the family meal, which was spread out in the kitchen. The inhabitants of Wet Waste were primitive people, with the frank, unabashed manner that flourishes still in lonely places, especially in the wilds of Yorkshire; but I had no idea that in these days of penny posts and cheap newspapers such entire ignorance of the outer world could have existed in any corner, however remote, of Great Britain.

When I took one of the neighbour's children on my knee—a pretty little girl with the palest aureole of flaxen hair I had ever seen—and began to draw pictures for her of the birds and beasts of other countries, I was instantly surrounded by a crowd of children, and even grown-up people, while others came to their doorways and looked on from a distance, calling to each other in the strident unknown tongue which I have since discovered goes by the name of "Broad Yorkshire".

The following morning, as I came out of my room, I perceived that something was amiss in the village. A buzz of voices reached me as I passed the bar, and in the next house I could hear through the open window a high-pitched wail of lamentation.

The woman who brought me my breakfast was in tears, and in answer to my questions, told me that the neighbour's child, the little girl whom I had taken on my knee the evening before, had died in the night.

I felt sorry for the general grief that the little creature's death seemed to arouse, and the uncontrolled wailing of the poor mother took my appetite away.

I hurried off early to my work, calling on my way for the keys, and with Brian for my companion descended once more into the crypt, and drew and measured with an absorption that gave me no time that day to listen for sounds real or fancied. Brian, too, on this occasion seemed quite content, and slept peacefully beside me on the stone floor. When I had worked as long as I could, I put away my books with regret that even then I had not quite finished, as I had hoped to do. It would be necessary come again for a short time on the morrow. When I returned the keys late that afternoon, the old clergyman met me at the door, and asked me to come in and have tea with him.

"And has the work prospered?" he asked, as we sat down in the long, low room, into which I had just been ushered, and where he seemed to live entirely.

I told him it had, and showed it to him.

"You have seen the original, of course?" I said.

"Once," he replied, gazing fixedly at it. He evidently did not care to be communicative, so I turned the conversation to the age of the church.

"All here is old," he said. "When I was young, forty years ago, and came here because I had no means of mine own, and was much moved to marry at that time, I felt oppressed that all was so old; and that this place was so far removed from the world, for which I had at times longing grievous to be borne; but I had chosen my lot, and with it I was forced be content. My son, marry not in youth, for love, which truly in that season is a mighty power, turns away the heart from study, and young children break the back of ambition. Neither marry in middle life, when woman is seen to be but a woman and her talk a weariness, so you will not be burdened with a wife in your old age."

I had my own views on the subject of marriage, for I am of opinion that a well-chosen companion of domestic tastes and docile and devoted temperament may be of material assistance to a professional man. But my opinions once formulated, it is not of moment to me to discuss them with others, so I changed the subject, and asked if the neighbouring villages were as antiquated as Wet Waste.

"Yes, all about here is old," he repeated. "The paved road leading to Dyke Fens is an ancient pack road, made even in the time of the Romans. Dyke Fens, which is very near here, a matter of but four or five miles, is likewise old, and forgotten by the world. The Reformation never reached it. It stopped here. And at Dyke Fens they still have a priest and a bell, and bow down before the saints. It is a damnable heresy, and weekly I expound it as such to my people, showing them true doctrines; and I have heard that this same priest has so far yielded himself to the Evil One that he has preached against me as withholding gospel truths from my flock; but I take no heed of it, neither of his pamphlet touching the Clementine Homilies, in which he vainly contradicts that which I have plainly set forth and proven beyond doubt, concerning the word Asaph."

The old man was fairly off on his favourite subject, and it was some time before I could get away. As it was, he followed me to the door, and I only escaped because the old clerk hobbled up at that moment, and claimed his attention.

The following morning I went for the keys for the third and last time. I had decided to leave early the next day. I was tired of Wet Waste, and a certain gloom seemed to my fancy to be gathering over the place. There was a sensation of trouble in the air, as if, although the day was bright and clear, a storm were coming.

This morning, to my astonishment, the keys were refused to me when I asked for them. I did not, however, take the refusal as final—I make it a rule never to take a refusal as final—and after a short delay I was shown into the room where, as usual, the clergyman was sitting, or rather, on this occasion, was walking up and down.

"My son," he said with vehemence, "I know wherefore you have come, but it is of no avail. I cannot lend the keys again."

I replied that, on the contrary, I hoped he would give them to me at once.

"It is impossible," he repeated. "I did wrong, exceeding wrong. I will never part with them again."

"Why not?"

He hesitated, and then said slowly:

"The old clerk, Abraham Kelly, died last night." He paused, and then went on: "The doctor has just been here to tell me of that which is a mystery to him. I do not wish the people of the place to know it, and only to me he has mentioned it, but he has discovered plainly on the throat of the old man, and also, but more faintly on the child's, marks as of strangulation. None but he has observed it, and he is at a loss how to account for it. I, alas! can account for it but in one way, but in one way!"

I did not see what all this had to do with the crypt, but to humour the old man, I asked what that way was.

"It is a long story, and, haply, to a stranger it may appear but foolishness, but I will even tell it; for I perceive that unless I furnish a reason for withholding the keys, you will not cease to entreat me for them.

"I told you at first when you inquired of me concerning the crypt, that it had been closed these thirty years, and so it was. Thirty years ago a certain Sir Roger Despard departed this life, even the Lord of the manor of Wet Waste and Dyke Fens, the last of his family, which is now, thank the Lord, extinct. He was a man of a vile life, neither fearing God nor regarding man, nor having compassion on innocence, and the Lord appeared to have given him over to the tormentors even in this world, for he suffered many things of his vices, more especially from drunkenness, in which seasons, and they were many, he was as one possessed by seven devils, being an abomination to his household and a root of bitterness to all, both high and low.

"And, at last, the cup of his iniquity being full to the brim, he came to die, and I went to exhort him on his death-bed; for I heard that terror had come upon him, and that evil imaginations encompassed him so thick on every side, that few of them that were with him could abide in his presence. But when I saw him I perceived that there was no place of repentance left for him, and he scoffed at me and my superstition, even as he lay dying, and swore there was no God and no angel, and all were damned even as he was. And the next day, towards evening, the pains of death came upon him, and he raved the more exceedingly, inasmuch as he said he was being strangled by the Evil One. Now on his table was his hunting knife, and with his last strength he crept and laid hold upon it, no man withstanding him, and swore a great oath that if he went down to burn in hell, he would leave one of his hands behind on earth, and that it would never rest until it had drawn blood from the throat of another and strangled him, even as he himself was being strangled. And he cut off his own right hand at the wrist, and no man dared go near him to stop him, and the blood went through the floor, even down to the ceiling of the room below, and thereupon he died.

"And they called me in the night, and told me of his oath, and I counselled that no man should speak of it, and I took the dead hand, which none had ventured to touch, and I laid it beside him in his coffin; for I thought it better he should take it with him, so that he might have it, if haply some day after much tribulation he should perchance be moved to stretch forth his hands towards God. But the story got spread about, and the people were affrighted, so, when he came to be buried in the place of his fathers, he being the last of his family, and the crypt likewise full, I had it closed, and kept the keys myself, and suffered no man to enter therein any more; for truly he was a man of an evil life, and the devil is not yet wholly overcome, nor cast chained into the lake of fire. So in time the story died out, for in thirty years much is forgotten. And when you came and asked me for the keys, I was at the first minded to withhold them; but I thought it was a vain superstition, and I perceived that you do but ask a second time for what is first refused; so I let you have them, seeing it was not an idle curiosity, but a desire to improve the talent committed to you, that led you to require them."

The old man stopped, and I remained silent, wondering what would be the best way to get them just once more.

"Surely, sir," I said at last, "one so cultivated and deeply read as yourself cannot be biased by an idle superstition."

"I trust not," he replied, "and yet—it is a strange thing that since the crypt was opened two people have died, and the mark is plain upon the throat of the old man and visible on the young child. No blood was drawn, but the second time the grip was stronger than the first. The third time, perchance—"

"Superstition such as that," I said with authority, "is an entire want of faith in God. You once said so yourself."

I took a high moral tone which is often efficacious with conscientious, humble-minded people.

He agreed, and accused himself of not having faith as a grain of mustard seed; but even when I had got him so far as that, I had a severe struggle for the keys. It was only when I finally explained to him that if any malign influence had been let loose the first day, at any rate, it was out now for good or evil, and no further going or coming of mine could make any difference, that I finally gained my point. I was young, and he was old; and, being much shaken by what had occurred, he gave way at last, and I wrested the keys from him.

I will not deny that I went down the steps that day with a vague, indefinable repugnance, which was only accentuated by the closing of the two doors behind me. I remembered then, for the first time, the faint jangling of the key and other sounds which I had noticed the first day, and how one of the skulls had fallen. I went to the place where it still lay. I have already said these walls of skulls were built up so high as to be within a few inches of the top of the low archways that led into more distant portions of the vault. The displacement of the skull in question had left a small hole just large enough for me to put my hand through. I noticed for the first time, over the archway above it, a carved coat-of-arms, and the name, now almost obliterated, of Despard. This, no doubt, was the Despard vault. I could not resist moving a few more skulls and looking in, holding my candle as near the aperture as I could. The vault was full. Piled high, one upon another, were old coffins, and remnants of coffins, and strewn bones. I attribute my present determination to be cremated to the painful impression produced on me by this spectacle. The coffin nearest the archway alone was intact, save for a large crack across the lid. I could not get a ray from my candle to fall on the brass plates, but I felt no doubt this was the coffin of the wicked Sir Roger. I put back the skulls, including the one which had rolled down, and carefully finished my work. I was not there much more than an hour, but I was glad to get away.

If I could have left Wet Waste at once I should have done so, for I had a totally unreasonable longing to leave the place; but I found that only one train stopped during the day at the station from which I had come, and that it would not be possible to be in time for it that day.

Accordingly I submitted to the inevitable, and wandered about with Brian for the remainder of the afternoon and until late in the evening, sketching and smoking. The day was oppressively hot, and even after the sun had set across the burnt stretches of the wolds, it seemed to grow very little cooler. Not a breath stirred. In the evening, when I was tired of loitering in the lanes, I went up to my own room, and after contemplating afresh my finished study of the fresco, I suddenly set to work to write the part of my paper bearing upon it. As a rule, I write with difficulty, but that evening words came to me with winged speed, and with them a hovering impression that I must make haste, that I was much pressed for time. I wrote and wrote, until my candles guttered out and left me trying to finish by the moonlight, which, until I endeavoured to write by it, seemed as clear as day.

I had to put away my MS., and, feeling it was too early to go to bed, for the church clock was just counting out ten, I sat down by the open window and leaned out to try and catch a breath of air. It was a night of exceptional beauty; and as I looked out my nervous haste and hurry of mind were allayed. The moon, a perfect circle, was—if so poetic an expression be permissible—as it were, sailing across a calm sky. Every detail of the little village was as clearly illuminated by its beams as if it were broad day; so, also, was the adjacent church with its primeval yews, while even the wolds beyond were dimly indicated, as if through tracing paper.

I sat a long time leaning against the window-sill. The heat was still intense. I am not, as a rule, easily elated or readily cast down; but as I sat that night in the lonely village on the moors, with Brian's head against my knee, how, or why, I know not, a great depression gradually came upon me.

My mind went back to the crypt and the countless dead who had been laid there. The sight of the goal to which all human life, and strength, and beauty, travel in the end, had not affected me at the time, but now the very air about me seemed heavy with death.

What was the good, I asked myself, of working and toiling, and grinding down my heart and youth in the mill of long and strenuous effort, seeing that in the grave folly and talent, idleness and labour lie together, and are alike forgotten? Labour seemed to stretch before me till my heart ached to think of it, to stretch before me even to the end of life, and then came, as the recompense of my labour—the grave. Even if I succeeded, if, after wearing my life threadbare with toll, I succeeded, what remained to me in the end? The grave. A little sooner, while the hands and eyes were still strong to labour, or a little later, when all power and vision had been taken from them; sooner or later only—the grave.

I do not apologise for the excessively morbid tenor of these reflections, as I hold that they were caused by the lunar effects which I have endeavoured to transcribe. The moon in its various quarterings has always exerted a marked influence on what I may call the sub-dominant, namely, the poetic side of my nature.

I roused myself at last, when the moon came to look in upon me where I sat, and, leaving the window open, I pulled myself together and went to bed.

I fell asleep almost immediately, but I do not fancy I could have been asleep very long when I was wakened by Brian. He was growling in a low, muffled tone, as he sometimes did in his sleep, when his nose was buried in his rug. I called out to him to shut up; and as he did not do so, turned in bed to find my match box or something to throw at him. The moonlight was still in the room, and as I looked at him I saw him raise his head and evidently wake up. I admonished him, and was just on the point of falling asleep when hie began to growl again in a low, savage manner that waked me most effectually. Presently he shook himself and got up, and began prowling about the room. I sat up in bed and called to him, but he paid no attention. Suddenly I saw him stop short in the moonlight;

he showed his teeth, and crouched down, his eyes following something in the air. I looked at him in horror. Was he going mad? His eyes were glaring, and his head moved slightly as if he were following the rapid movements of an enemy. Then, with a furious snarl, he suddenly sprang from the ground, and rushed in great leaps across the room towards me, dashing himself against the furniture, his eyes rolling, snatching and tearing wildly in the air with his teeth. I saw he had gone mad. I leaped out of bed, and rushing at him, caught him by the throat. The moon had gone behind a cloud; but in the darkness I felt him turn upon me, felt him rise up, and his teeth close in my throat. I was being strangled. With all the strength of despair, I kept my grip of his neck, and, dragging him across the room, tried to crush in his head against the iron rail of my bedstead. It was my only chance. I felt the blood running down my neck. I was suffocating. After one moment of frightful struggle, I beat his head against the bar and heard his skull give way. I felt him give one strong shudder, a groan, and then I fainted away.

* * * * * *

When I came to myself I was lying on the floor, surrounded by the people of the house, my reddened hands still clutching Brian's throat. Someone was holding a candle towards me, and the draught from the window made it flare and waver. I looked at Brian. He was stone dead. The blood from his battered head was trickling slowly over my hands. His great jaw was fixed in something that— in the uncertain light—I could not see.

They turned the light a little.

"Oh, God!" I shrieked. "There! Look! Look!"

"He's off his head," said some one, and I fainted again.

* * * * * *

I was ill for about a fortnight without regaining consciousness, a waste of time of which even now I cannot think without poignant regret. When I did recover consciousness, I found I was being carefully nursed by the old clergyman and the people of the house. I have often heard the unkindness of the world in general inveighed against, but for my part I can honestly say that I have received many more kindnesses than I have time to repay. Country people especially are remarkably attentive to strangers in illness.

I could not rest until I had seen the doctor who attended me, and had received his assurance that I should be equal to reading my paper on the appointed day. This pressing anxiety removed, I told him of what I had seen before I fainted the second time. He listened attentively, and then assured me, in a manner that was intended to be soothing, that I was suffering from an hallucination, due, no doubt, to the shock of my dog's sudden madness.

"Did you see the dog after it was dead?" I asked. He said he did. The whole jaw was covered with blood and foam; the teeth certainly seemed convulsively fixed, but the case being evidently one of extraordinarily virulent hydrophobia, owing to the intense heat, he had had the body buried immediately.

* * * * * *

My companion stopped speaking as we reached our lodgings, and went upstairs. Then, lighting a candle, he slowly turned down his collar.

"You see I have the marks still," he said, "but I have no fear of dying of hydrophobia. I am told such peculiar scars could not have been made by the teeth of a dog. If you look closely you see the pressure of the five fingers. That is the reason why I wear high collars."

Also published by ReScript Books...

The Ivory Gate:
Later Poems & Fragments
Thomas Lovell Beddoes

THOMAS LOVELL BEDDOES (1803-1849) was an English poet and dramatist whose early play *The Brides' Tragedy* was highly praised. He studied medicine at the Universities of Göttingen and Würzburg, where his involvement in radical politics led to his deportation. He spent the rest of his life in Switzerland and Germany, continuing to write but showing only occasional and fleeting interest in publication. His celebrated drama *Death's Jest-Book* and his *Collected Poems* were published posthumously.

This volume, edited and with an introduction by Alan Halsey, makes available separately for the first time the surviving text and fragments of Beddoes' unfinished work *The Ivory Gate*, together with a collection of his later poetry.

ReScript Books, 2011, ISBN 978-1-874400-50-9, UK price £9.00